ELEVATOR ENCOUNTERS

CAITLYN LYNCH

Caitlyn Lynch

ELEVATOR ENCOUNTERS

The stories in the book were originally published as three short ebook novellas, *Ellie's Encounter*, *Juliet's Romeo* and *The Best Man For Leah*. *The Best Man For Leah* has previously only been available as part of the Just You And Me box set.

Caitlyn Lynch

Other Works by The Author

DANA'S DUO

RANGER HEAT SERIES
1.   FIRST SUBMISSION
2.   SECOND SURRENDER
3.   THIRD THRILLS

SUNFISH ISLAND RESORT SERIES
1.   FINDING CORY
(INCLUDED IN THE TROPICAL TRYST
BOX SET)

2.   THE RELUCTANT BILLIONAIRE
(INCLUDED IN THE BILLIONAIRE
EVER AFTER BOX SET)

SHENANIGANS PRESS ANTHOLOGIES
STOCKING STUFFERS
RED HOTS
SUMMER HEAT

HALLOWEEN ANTHOLOGY (upcoming)

Caitlyn Lynch

CONTENTS

Caitlyn Lynch

Ellie's Encounter

"Hold the lift!"

Jacob stuck a foot out automatically and the doors slid closed on it, opening again a moment later with a protesting *ping*.

"Thank you!" a young woman slipped through the widening gap, smiling up at him. He couldn't help but give her an appreciative look and down; she was a sight for sore eyes, a pretty little thing with big hazel eyes and silky brown hair tumbling past her shoulders. She was wearing a pale gray business suit that looked a little the worse for wear, creased and sagging.

"What floor?" Jacob asked pleasantly.

"Hm? Oh. Uh, the eleventh," she looked at the key card folder clutched in her hand. "Please," she added as an afterthought, leaning back against the elevator car's paneled sides.

"Sure," Jacob punched the button, leaned against the other side of the car and surveyed her thoughtfully. "Y'all must be English, with that accent," he said. "You called it a *lift*, too. Just flew in, huh?"

*

Ellie forced her weary eyes open and peered back at the tall cowboy she'd found herself sharing the lift with. She'd instantly classified him as a cowboy based on the black hat, jeans and boots; a second look did nothing to dispel the impression. It did tell her that he was a very *handsome* cowboy, though, the smile quirking his tanned face showing straight white teeth and a really rather adorable dimple in his chin. He towered over her, or would if he wasn't slouching casually back against the wall. Her eyes tracked down, slid over broad shoulders straining at the seams of his faded-blue chambray shirt, down over his chest and flat stomach, to the strong thighs shown off to excellent advantage by his close-fitting jeans.

"Yes," she said finally, in answer to his question. "Just flew in."

"Here for the big writers' conference?"

"That's right," she nodded, looking at him curiously. "Are you?"

"Yeah, but I'm not a writer." He smiled self-deprecatingly. "My mom is Patsy Bain; she brought me along to be her gofer."

"Patsy Bain!" Ellie's tired eyes snapped wide open. "She's the keynote speaker!" *Because she's wildly successful*, she didn't say out loud. *Obviously her son would know that.* She was just about to open her mouth again to beg him to introduce her to Patsy when the lift suddenly shuddered and stopped dead.

"What the..?" Jacob muttered, punched a couple of buttons on the control panel. The elevator was old but the control panel had been remodeled, had a display showing the floor number. It was stuck in between 7 and 8.

The lights flickered.

"Oh, *no*," Ellie said, just before the lights went out and they were plunged into darkness.

"Don't panic," Jacob said, pulling his phone out and tapping the screen. The bluish light that promptly brightened the elevator showed him that his companion didn't look reassured; she was looking frantically around for some means of escape. "Take it easy, miss." He looked back at the control panel, found the alarm button and pressed it. There was a loud ringing sound and a small emergency light began to glow.

"Hello?" a voice said tinnily through the small speaker a moment later. "Is anyone there?"

"Yes, we're stuck in the elevator," Jacob said a little irritably.

"Can you tell me the reference number, please? You're through to the central control room. We'll have a diagnostician check out the issue…"

"Okay." Jacob read off the number stamped into the brass control panel just above the alarm button. There was a brief silence before the tinny voice said;

"You're in the Westlake Hotel on East 56th Street, aren't you?" The voice sounded rather resigned, Jacob thought.

"Yup. Stuck between the seventh and eighth floors, it looks like."

"We'll get a technician out to you but it'll be at least an hour. Are you in there alone, sir?"

"No, there's a lady with me." Jacob glanced at his companion, alarmed to see her looking a little pale, clinging to the brass rail at the side of the elevator tightly.

"Of course there is."

"Excuse me?"

"Nothing, sir. As I said, it will be at least an hour before the repair technician arrives, so please just remain calm and wait. The line will close now; please press the alarm button again if you need to speak with me again."

There wasn't a lot he could say but "Okay."

*

"We're stuck in here," Ellie said miserably into the silence that followed. At least the small emergency light had stayed on when the line went silent, meaning the cowboy could put his phone away.

"I'm afraid so. Might as well get comfortable." He held something out towards her; she blinked before recognizing it as a large takeout coffee cup. "This'll be cold by the time we get out, I'll have to go fetch Mom another one. Don't suppose you happen to like soy chai latte?"

"Not especially, but if it's all we've got to drink I guess I wouldn't mind so much," Ellie said with a sigh, accepting the cup and taking a sip. "Thank you."

Broad shoulders lifted in a shrug. "You're welcome. I'm Jacob Bainbridge, by the way."

"Eleanor Scott. Ellie." She handed the cup back.

"Guess we might as well get comfortable, eh?" He bent his knees and slid gracefully down to sit on the floor, making the motion look far too easy in Ellie's opinion. She certainly couldn't do the same thing, her skirt would ride up too far anyway. She cursed her own decision to wear a skirt suit to travel, but she'd been hoping to maybe score a free business class upgrade if she looked like a business traveler. Forlorn hope *that* had been. She wished now that she'd just worn her comfy tracksuit pants and a T-shirt.

Awkwardly, she knelt and then shuffled around to sit, back against the hard wooden paneling. Her shoes were hurting her feet so she toed them off, hoping that her feet didn't smell.

"So is that the name you write under, Ellie Scott?" Jacob asked after a few moments of silence.

She was quite sure that her scalding blush was visible even in the faint emergency light. "No… no, that's my real name. I write under a pseudonym."

"Which is…?"

"I'd, um, rather not say." *Shouldn't have told him your real name in the first place, you idiot,* she silently castigated herself. *Far better if everyone here knows you only as Barbie Belle.* She was blaming the jet lag for that slip of the tongue, definitely.

"Oh," Jacob gave her a knowing look. "You're an erotica writer."

"Yes, and I fully intended not to tell anyone here my real name, so please…?" she gave him a hopeful look.

"My lips are sealed, darlin'," he mimed locking them before grinning cheekily at her. Unable to resist his charm, she smiled back.

"Thanks."

He offered her the coffee cup and she took another sip, unable to suppress a grimace at the taste. "That's really your mother's favorite? It seems terribly… I don't know, *bland*, for Patsy Bain?"

That made Jacob chuckle. "Sadly, Mom is lactose intolerant. And while she would really have liked a double shot of espresso, I'm cuttin' off her caffeine for the day before she starts bouncin' off the walls."

That made Ellie giggle. "You mean thing!"

"She's had about six cups, don't go thinkin' she's dying of withdrawal, now." His grin was slow, charming. Ellie was glad she was sitting down because otherwise she suspected that her knees might have melted.

"Still, bringing along a gofer who takes it upon themselves to ration your caffeine intake seems unwise," she pointed out. "Especially for writers. Most of us run on coffee anyway."

"Don't I know it." He took the cup back, took a sip and made a face. "Ugh. You're right, it's disgusting."

"I didn't say that!" Ellie pointed out, half-laughing.

"Naw, 'spose you didn't." He sighed, putting the cup down on the floor, reaching up to take his hat off and pass his hand over short blond hair, scratching lightly at his scalp. "So what you do when you're not writing, Ellie? Or are you full-time? You must be doin' all right, to have flown over here for the conference…"

"Doing all right, yes, but not well enough to give up my day job. I'm a legal secretary."

"Yeah?" he nodded. "Bet you're a quick typist then."

"Very." Talking to him was helping to distract Ellie from the nerve-wracking feeling that the walls were closing in, but as he fell briefly silent she couldn't quite help herself from looking up and around, her fingers digging into the soft carpet on the floor.

"Are you alright, Ellie?" Jacob asked quietly.

"I'm a little bit claustrophobic," she confessed. "I don't like lifts at the best of times, but with my room on the eleventh floor I just didn't feel up to climbing all those flights of stairs."

"Aw, hell, you gonna be okay?" His eyes were very blue, kind and sympathetic. "Can't say I'm all that fond of enclosed places myself."

"Well, you are a cowboy," Ellie said, imagining that he was probably most in his element on the back of a horse under wide blue skies.

To her surprise, Jacob threw his head back and laughed heartily. "No. No I'm not," he admitted once he got control of himself again. "This," he plucked at his chambray shirt, indicated the hat beside his leg, "is yet another favor for my mom. The hero of her new book is a cowboy, and she convinced me to dress up to be a, a, I guess a *prop* for her."

Ellie found herself chuckling too. "You must really love your mom."

"She's a helluva lady."

"So what *do* you do?" Ellie pressed, curious about him now.

"I'm an architect," he smiled a little ruefully, flashing that adorable dimple in his chin again. "It's not nearly as sexy as a cowboy, I'm afraid."

"Better paying though, I'm sure," Ellie said astutely.

"I'm gettin' by."

From his smile she suspected that was an understatement, that he was in fact probably quite successful. Successful enough to be able to take a long weekend off to humor his mother at a romance writers' conference in New York City, at any rate. She sighed, glanced at her watch, but she hadn't checked what time it was when the elevator broke down.

"How long has it been, anyway?" she asked plaintively. "It must have been at least half an hour."

Jacob's expression was a little pitying. "It's been just about five minutes."

*

Ellie stared at Jacob in horror. "Five minutes? That's *all?*"

"I'm afraid so." He picked up the coffee cup, offered it again, but she shook her head.

"No. No thanks. I don't need to add 'need the bathroom' to my litany of woes."

Jacob smiled sympathetically before setting the cup down again. "Good call."

Silence fell between them then, Jacob leaning back against the side of the elevator and settling in to wait patiently. He found himself watching Ellie covertly, admiring her, the neat way she sat with her ankles crossed and her hands folded in her lap. Although her fingers were gripping each other tightly, he realized, spotting the whiteness of her knuckles. Gaze sliding back up to her face, he realized that she was pale, tiny beads of sweat standing out on her upper lip, her eyes glazed over as she breathed quickly.

*

Unable to escape the sensation that the walls were closing in, Ellie tried to keep her breathing steady, but quickly realized that she was failing badly. She had to close her eyes after a while, feeling a little dizzy.

"Ellie," Jacob's deep voice said. "You okay?" She heard him move, and after a moment a large warm hand closed over hers. "Whoa, your hands are freezing!" He settled to sit beside her, a large shoulder just brushing hers lightly, took both her hands between his large ones and chafed them lightly, trying to warm them. "Just breathe."

She opened her eyes and looked up at him, surprised to find him closer than she'd thought, looking down at her with concern in eyes that, she noticed for the first time, were an absolutely stunning shade of deep blue. Her gaze fell to his lips without even really thinking about it, and a blush spread across her cheeks as she noted how firm his mouth was, how full his lower lip. Unbidden, a fantasy of biting down on that lip while she straddled his lap, rubbing her breasts against his broad chest, slipped into her mind, distracting her briefly from their situation.

"Ellie?" Jacob questioned as she looked up at him from wide hazel eyes. She promptly blushed a quite charming shade of pink. Her tongue swiped over her parted lips, drawing his gaze down to her mouth. "Um," he forgot briefly what he'd planned to say. "Wow, you sure are pretty," somehow slipped out instead.

Ellie's cheeks flushed further, but she didn't drop her gaze. "The view's looking pretty good from here too," she agreed. "I'm very glad I'm not on my own stuck in here. That you're with me."

"I'm glad I'm stuck in here with you too," Jacob said dumbly. He couldn't stop looking at her mouth, at the way her lips moved as she spoke, her crisp accent washing over him. "We're going to be stuck in here for quite a while yet."

"And the time's passing really slowly," Ellie agreed, nodding. She hesitated briefly before asking "You married, or anything like that?"

"Quite single. You? You got a partner back in England who helps you figure out the scenarios for your books?"

"No!" she laughed. Chewed nervously on her lip until Jacob leaned forward. His breath played over her lips for a long moment, giving her ample time to move back, to pull away.

Ellie stayed right where she was until his mouth came down on hers.

*

Jacob's mouth was warm, his lips soft and gentle at first, then pressing more firmly as she parted her lips to flick her tongue against his. Long, capable fingers came up to curve against the side of her neck, his fingertips sliding into her hair at her nape, massaging sensuously.

Ellie moaned softly against Jacob's mouth; he certainly knew how to kiss, his tongue playing a teasing game with hers, tempting her to want more, to *take* more. Impatient suddenly, she moved, going to her knees and scrambling astride his lap. He smiled as she leaned back in to kiss him again, his hands landing on her thighs and sliding up, under the hem of the skirt which had already ridden up as she straddled him. His fingers stuttered as he encountered the lacy band high on her thigh.

"Stockings?" he murmured against her lips. "Who wears stockings on a transatlantic flight?"

"They're thigh-highs. And I do, because I wanted to look smart but can't stand how sweaty tights make me feel."

That made him chuckle, but she quieted him with her tongue slipping between his lips, felt his hands slide up further to cup her ass and squeeze, rolling her against him. He was most definitely into what they were doing, she realized, his cock hardening and rubbing against her through his jeans and the thin fabric of her panties. He was hitting on just the right spot, too, the stiff seam of his jeans rubbing over her clit making Ellie shake and moan into his mouth.

"Mm," Jacob pulled his lips from hers, started kissing down her throat.

Ellie made a pleasured little sound too, tipped her head back to give him better access, her eyes half-closing - and then she spotted something that made her go completely rigid.

"Ellie?" Jacob lifted his head, realizing at once that something wasn't right.

"Camera," she said stupidly, but he understood immediately, following the direction of her gaze to the video camera mounted in an upper corner of the elevator.

"I got it." Gently, he eased her off his lap, back down to sit on the floor, and stood up, unbuttoning his chambray shirt and pulling it off to reveal a hard-muscled, beautifully sculpted torso that had Ellie gasping at the sight, a sudden surge of lust nearly overwhelming her. Reaching up, Jacob hung the shirt neatly on the camera mount, completely obscuring the lens. "There we go." Grinning down at Ellie, he knelt back down beside her. "Now. Where were we?"

She reached out a hand to stay him as he reached for her again. "We were kissing, but I just need a minute to admire that seriously hot body you just oh-so-casually revealed."

Laughing, Jacob sat back on his haunches, deliberately flexed his biceps and pectoral muscles at her.

"No, seriously, how does an architect get muscles like that?" Ellie's gaze traced over him slowly, taking in every inch, from the perfectly defined six-pack to the bulging chest and arm muscles. He didn't look sculpted, though, not like a guy who spent all his spare hours in the gym. She waited curiously for his answer.

"Building," Jacob said succinctly. "My specialty is actually redesign and rebuild of heritage homes; I restore them myself. Blocks and wooden beams are pretty heavy, y'know, hauling them around keeps me in shape. Plus, I was a swimmer all through college; not national standard but pretty good."

"Well, that explains quite a lot." Ellie was still drinking him in with her eyes. Looking up to meet his, she smiled shyly. "For all I write about hot guys in my books, I've certainly never been trapped in an enclosed space with one even half as sexy as you."

Jacob looked pleased at that, reached out to her again. "Gettin' stuck in here with you feels like something straight out of a fantasy for me too, let me tell you."

She let him pull her back astride his lap, but this time he reached for the buttons of her blouse instead of putting his hands on her thighs, glancing at her questioningly. "This okay?"

"I suppose so," Ellie smiled shyly, unable to resist putting her hands on his shoulders, exploring the heavy muscles, the texture of his skin. He felt warm as she traced her fingertips lightly across his collarbone, up the strong line of his throat. "Seems only fair."

"That right?" His fingers were sure and deft as he worked the tiny buttons open quickly, spreading the blouse open, pushing it and her jacket back off her shoulders until she had to drop her hands to shrug the clothes off and discard them on the floor. Jacob hummed with approval at the sight of her breasts, barely covered by sheer pink lace. "Pretty."

"Erotica writers are all about secrets, you know." Ellie gave him a cheeky smirk, pleased with her own decision to only pack her prettiest underthings for this trip. They made her feel more confident, just knowing that the silk and lace was against her skin, and the look in Jacob's eyes was extremely flattering as he gazed reverently at her breasts.

"I like your secrets. Come up here, gorgeous…" a strong arm curling around her waist lifted her up against him, and he bent his head to press his face into her cleavage, mouthing at the soft skin swelling from the upper edge of one lacy cup.

Ellie closed her eyes blissfully and relaxed into Jacob's caresses, enjoying the sensations as he kissed and mouthed at her breasts, hot mouth dampening the thin lace. She let out a soft little cry of pleasure as he suckled her nipple into his mouth, working it roughly with his tongue.

Jacob had to restrain the urge to cry out himself as Ellie's fingers speared into his hair, nails scratching sensually at his scalp. She was soft and yielding in his arms, pure temptation, the faint scent of vanilla and roses still rising from her skin despite her long day of traveling. Her nipple hardened in his mouth as he suckled, her hips tilting forward to press closer.

An hour, he thought, *an hour at least before the repair guy gets here*. It wouldn't be enough for what he really wanted, for that he would need hours and hours to leisurely explore Ellie's beautiful body in a comfortable bed, but it would have to suffice, for now at least. He held her close with one hand on her waist and ran the other up the softness of her thigh, tracing around the top of her stocking before slowly moving up to cup her ass. Letting her nipple out of his mouth, he kissed up her chest, nibbling lightly at her collarbone as his hand slid around the rich curve and into her cleft.

The heat he found there, the dampness when his fingers pressed against the lacy panties he was sure would match her bra, had Jacob's cock swelling to full attention. Just the thought of getting inside Ellie, of feeling her silky juices coating his cock as he drove deep, made him groan deep in his throat with need.

*

Ellie clung to Jacob, little pants and gasps spilling from her lips as one strong hand lifted her up towards him and the fingers of the other slipped under the soft curve of her ass, up into her cleft, edging her damp panties aside.

"Wet," he whispered against her neck, "I like that." His fingers were deft, certain, fingertips circling her clit slowly.

"Oh God," Ellie said aloud, fingers tightening in his hair, tugging at it, though he didn't seem to care.

"Like that, huh?" Jacob murmured knowingly, fingers circling a little faster. "This should help you relax a bit."

"Ungh," she mumbled incoherently as he started sucking a slow, moist love bite onto her collarbone. She was very far from relaxed right then, the tension in her body twisting higher and higher until she felt like a clockwork mechanism wound too tight.

"You gonna come for me, sweetheart?" His voice was low, sensually knowing as Ellie began to tremble.

"Please," was the only word she could make herself utter, her breath coming in frantic little pants as her head tipped back and her eyes closed. The familiar warm tingle in her crotch built steadily as Jacob's fingers worked, and as he shifted his hand slightly and pushed a thick thumb slowly up into her pussy, the climax spread through her whole body, making her shake and moan loudly.

"That's it," Jacob whispered as Ellie practically melted in his arms, soft and yielding, her pussy dragging on his thumb in little fluttering pulses as the orgasm went on and on. "That's it, sweetheart. Beautiful. *Beautiful.*"

She went completely limp against him with a soft gasp, dropping down to rest her forehead against his shoulder, and he gently eased his hand out of her panties and lowered her down to rest on his lap. They sat like that for several minutes as Ellie's breathing slowly returned to normal, though Jacob could still feel her heart beating quickly. He didn't say anything, just nuzzled against her hair quietly until she lifted her head to look at him.

"Well," Ellie had to struggle to keep her voice steady as she met Jacob's eyes, "that was nicely distracting. Thank you."

"My pleasure."

"I think it was all mine, actually." Deliberately, she wiggled in his lap, rubbing against his aching erection. "You haven't had yours yet."

"Yeah, I wasn't the one on the verge of a panic attack."

Jacob smiled with his eyes as much as his lips, Ellie noticed, the corners of them crinkling in a way that made her insides turn to absolute mush. "I think you staved it off successfully," she said a little vaguely, gazing dreamily into those deep blue eyes.

"You sure? If you're still feelin' a little stressed out, I got some more ideas to distract you," Jacob grinned roguishly, and Ellie laughed.

"If they're anything like as good as that, I'm down. I just," she nibbled at her lower lip a little uncertainly, glanced up at his shirt hanging over the camera, "I just don't want anyone to catch us? Public exhibitionism isn't really my thing…"

"Mine either." Jacob leaned sideways a little and tapped on the screen of his phone, lying disregarded by his hat on the floor. "But the lady at the call center said an hour, and it's still only been fifteen minutes."

"What?" Ellie's eyes widened comically, and Jacob had to stifle a laugh. "You're not serious!"

"See for yourself." He held the phone up, and she let out a groan of despair and slumped forward to rest her forehead on his bare shoulder.

"Fuck it then," she muttered against his neck. "I was going to suggest that we save anything else for a bed, but there's no way I can survive another forty-five minutes or more in here without jumping your sexy bones."

Jacob did laugh at that, and he moved his hand up her back to fiddle with her bra clip. "Sounds good to me," he said before unfastening the clip.

Ellie smiled against his shoulder as she felt her bra loosen, leaned back to shrug the straps down her arms and drop the bra aside. Jacob's gaze fastened on her breasts and he licked his lips.

"Helluva view," he muttered hoarsely.

Ellie could tell he really did appreciate the sight of her breasts, since his cock had just shoved hard at her through their clothes. Smiling, she reached down to take his hands, bringing them up to her chest before leaning back in to kiss him again.

Offered a double handful, Jacob was not about to protest. Ellie's nipples were hard as berries against his gently exploring fingers; she made a pleased little sound in her throat as he traced lightly around them before flicking quickly over them with his thumbs. She ground her hips against his as her tongue played a teasing game, and he couldn't take it any longer. Shifting quickly, he tipped her off his lap, down onto her back on the elevator floor, leaning down to fasten his mouth on one pouting nipple as his hand slipped back up her skirt again.

Ellie arched into Jacob's touch, moaning as he drew skilfully on her nipple, tongue wrapping around it. He was pushing her skirt up, tugging her panties down, and she was more than happy to let him. Her hands caressed his short-cropped hair and the back of his strong neck, his broad shoulders, as he nursed at her breast, suckling on her nipple until she couldn't suppress a small gasp of pain.

At once, Jacob let go, kissing the abused nipple gently a few times before moving across the other and repeating his actions, taking the time to learn just how much pressure Ellie liked. She didn't like it when he used the edge of his teeth, he soon found, but she moaned and trembled when he sucked in fast, throbbing pulses. Two fingers slid back into her soaked pussy again and she nearly shouted his name, clawing at his shoulders.

"You called?" Jacob lifted his head, grinned at her, his lips red from the pressure he'd been exerting on her nipples.

"Get your jeans off and fuck me," Ellie demanded breathlessly. "Come on, Jacob, please, you're driving me crazy!"

"Yeah?" he thrust his fingers slowly, thumb rubbing over her clit. "I can tell," he whispered, lowering his head to give her nipples a few more licks. "You're so wet, so slippery."

"Now!" she almost wailed, jack-knifing up and trying to grab at his pants. He laughed and backed off, sliding his fingers out of her regretfully and sitting back on his haunches to unfasten his belt and fly.

Ellie took the opportunity to unzip her skirt, rucked up to little more than an awkward belt around her waist, and kick free of it, leaving her wearing nothing but her thigh-high, lacy-topped stockings and high heels. Jacob groaned deeply at the sight, wrestling out of his boots and jeans awkwardly, suddenly feeling all thumbs.

"God damn, but you're beautiful, sweetheart; look at you! I keep thinking I'm having some sort of fantastic dream and I'm gonna wake up any minute, that the bubble's gonna burst and I'll realize you were only a fantasy."

"Better fuck me before that happens then," Ellie demanded, making grabby hands at him as he finally kicked free of his jeans.

"You okay down there?" he figured he'd better check; the floor was carpeted but it wasn't exactly plush, he didn't want her to get rug burns on her ass.

"Jacob!"

He chuckled at her impatience, but he didn't really feel inclined to delay either, not looking at her lying there with her arms and legs open, welcoming and warm. Her slick was a shiny snail's trail on her upper thighs above those fantasy-inducing stockings; he licked his lips, thought about going in for a taste, but his cock was aching way too much to wait any longer. Kneeling between her thighs, he slid his hands under her buttocks, lifting her ass off the floor a little way, lining his cock up with her soaked pussy. "You asked for it, you're gonna get it," he said roughly, and pushed deep with one long, slow thrust.

Ellie thrust the fingers of one hand into her mouth to try and suppress the wracking screams that sought to burst free; Jacob's cock felt absolutely amazing as he drove it right to the root inside her. She hadn't had much of a chance to look at him as he hastily stripped his pants off, but he'd certainly been sporting a healthy-sized bulge and he felt *more* than generously endowed as he seemed to keep thrusting deeper and deeper.

Ellie *yowled* against her silencing fingers, heard Jacob's rough chuckle as he finally stilled. "Make all the noise you want," he told her. "Pretty sure nobody can hear us." He reached forward and tweaked one nipple, tugging on it lightly, giving it a little twist. "Come on. I wanna hear you moan for me." His hips started to move again then, setting up a slow, rocking rhythm, driving steadily back and forth, his hand still on her ass holding her still as he fucked her.

It felt so good that Ellie's eyes just about rolled back in her head; she took her fingers out of her mouth and clawed with both hands at the rough carpet beneath her, searching for some sort of anchor to the real world as Jacob took her up to the clouds. He was praising her gruffly as his hips worked a slow grinding circle, his fingers letting go of her breast and dipping down between them to massage her clit again.

The climax was slower to build this time, the tingling rush spreading from her pussy out through her whole body, making Ellie's eyelids flutter and her toes curl as a low, continuous *aaahhhhh* sound escaped her lips.

"Ahh, *fuck*," Jacob groaned himself as Ellie's slick pussy sucked at him, contracting tightly as she came hard, her whole body shaking. "Fuck, sweetheart, that's so good!" He'd been determined to hold back, to have her come again, but now that she had he could let go, could pound into her still-clenching passage and take his own pleasure. Feeling his balls pull up tight, ready to explode his load deep inside her, he threw his head back and roared with ecstasy as the hot stream of cum flooded up his cock and into Ellie's quivering body. "Fuck," he muttered again, softer this time, "*fuck*, Ellie."

"Mm hmm, you did that," Ellie mumbled as he lowered her hips gently to the floor, curled over her to kiss her again. She curled her arms around his neck when he made to pull back, holding on tightly, and Jacob chuckled softly and rolled them both so that he was on the bottom and she lay atop him in a loose sprawl of relaxed limbs.

"You okay?" he checked quietly, smoothing her tangled hair back from her face.

"Mm hmm," she said again, nuzzling her face against his neck. "Save a horse, ride a cowboy and all that. Great ride. Highly recommended."

That made Jacob laugh, a deep rumble in his chest. He felt Ellie smile against his throat. "You do remember that I'm not really a cowboy?"

"Cowboy, architect, whatever," she gave an affected little sigh before leaning back, propping her forearms on his chest and looking down at him. "I might have to make the hero of my next story a sexy cowboy-architect."

"You do that, as long as he's getting involved with a legal secretary who writes erotica novels on the side and has lots of sexy secret kinks."

Ellie giggled at that. "Maybe." Flexing her knees, she slowly, reluctantly eased up, sighing with loss as Jacob's cock slid out of her. He sighed too, watching her reaching for her purse, finding a pack off tissues to clean up with.

It was then that Jacob realized he was lying on his cowboy hat. Cursing, he rolled to his side to pull it out, try to push it back into shape. Ellie snickered as she realized what he was doing.

"Oops." Her eyes were brimming with mischief as he looked over at her, and Jacob couldn't resist. Throwing the battered hat aside, he swooped in to tickle her.

"Totally your fault! I'll tell my mother that I was seduced in the elevator by a siren of an erotica writer. She either won't believe me or she'll write a book about it."

Giggling madly, Ellie sought to escape. "Hey, hey, she can't write a book about it, it's my idea!"

Grinning, he leaned in to kiss her again.

*

At that precise moment, the speaker in the elevator's control panel suddenly crackled to life. "This is the elevator repair technician, you there, sir?"

"Yes," Jacob hastily let go of Ellie and scrambled over to the panel, snagging his pants on the way. "We're here!"

"Good, good. Camera doesn't seem to be working, I just wanted to check I had the right elevator." There was a distinct undertone of amusement in the man's voice.

"Definitely the right elevator. How soon can you have us out of here?" Zipping his fly, Jacob glanced over his shoulder and was instantly distracted by the sight of Ellie shimmying back into her skirt. He stared open-mouthed, missed the repair technician's reply. Oh God, now she was putting her bra on, tucking her breasts back into the pink lace cups. Resolutely, Jacob turned his back. "Sorry, I didn't catch that?"

"About two minutes. This elevator, it always has the same fault. The Emergency Stop fuse keeps popping. Just got to bypass the circuit in the main control panel… there we go."

The lights suddenly flickered back and the elevator made a whining sound and jerked into motion.

"Shit, shit, shit," it was a mad scramble for both of them to get dressed, Jacob dragging his shirt off the camera and hastily buttoning himself back into it as Ellie frantically tried to smooth her hair and make herself look tidy. It was a good thing that the elevator was old and slow, because when it finally reached the ground floor and opened they were both just about presentable again.

"Afternoon," they were greeted by an elderly, smiling man in mechanic's overalls. He stepped into the elevator, opened the control panel, pulled out a glass fuse and inserted a new one. "There we go. All fixed."

"Won't it just pop again?" Ellie asked.

"Sure it will, miss, but who knows when. This old girl's behaved herself for nearly six months this time," he closed the panel and gave it a fatherly pat. "Time before that, it was only a week. We can't just bypass the fuse, unfortunately, because that would break the Emergency Stop button altogether and then she'd fail city code."

"I see," Jacob murmured.

"Now, what floor were you folks headed for? I'll ride up with you, make sure she behaves herself. She's got a funny habit of pulling this trick when there's a handsome young couple inside like yourselves." There was a distinct twinkle in the old man's eyes. Ellie had the distinct feeling that he knew exactly what they'd been up to.

"Eleven," she said.

"Twelve," Jacob put in.

"Oh, you're not together, then? She's a dreadful matchmaker. Funnily enough it's almost fifty years to the day that I met my Rosa in this very elevator."

"Really?" Fascinated, Ellie blinked.

"It was my very first day on the job. Got sent down here because they knew exactly what the fault would be." The old man smiled reminiscently. "An easy job for the new kid, you see. Rosa was stuck inside. She was *very* grateful for bein' rescued. We got married three months later."

"That's a lovely story," Ellie said, and somehow her hand found its way into Jacob's. He squeezed gently. "So the elevator had the same fault all the way back then and it's never been fixed in all the years since?"

"Had the same fault ever since the hotel was built way back in the nineteen-twenties, miss. This old elevator's been matchmakin' folks for nearly a hundred years."

The doors slid open then at the eleventh floor and Ellie nodded awkwardly, slipping her hand out of Jacob's. "Well. Thanks for getting us out, anyway. Bye, Jacob." She moved forward quickly, not looking at him.

"See you at the conference," Jacob called after her, not willing to let her go that easily. A quick smile was the only answer he got before the doors slid closed again.

"Should have asked for her phone number," the elevator technician told him, shaking his head.

"Don't worry about it," Jacob assured him. "I know where to find her."

"Well, make sure you do. The old girl sulks when her matchmaking fails."

*

Ellie closed the door behind her and leaned on it, breathing fast, tears pricking at the back of her eyes. She could hardly believe what she'd just done; had sex with a complete stranger in a lift, of all the crazy, reckless things to do!

The fact that it had been mind-blowingly *good* sex had no bearing on the matter, she chided herself as she pushed off the door and headed into the bathroom, turning the shower on full blast. Or that Jacob had been sexy, nice and an extraordinary lover.

"Stop it," Ellie ordered herself aloud as the memories of what she'd just done threatened to overwhelm her. Stripping her clothes off hastily, she stepped into the shower and tried to wash away the warm, tingling sensations that still lingered throughout her body. It didn't work, even when she turned the shower all the way down to ice cold. The way her nipples peaked in protest at the chill water only made her think of the way Jacob had drawn on them with teeth and tongue.

Finally she gave up, turning off the spray of water and drying off. *I'm being foolish*, she tried to tell herself. It was just sex. She'd likely never see Jacob again; they hadn't even exchanged phone numbers, and while he'd said he'd see her at the conference, she was booked in under her pseudonym and would have to spend the whole weekend manning her booth. Somehow she didn't see him hunting through a big conference center full of romance writers and fans for her.

"Write it off to experience," Ellie told herself. "Literally." Her suitcase had been delivered to her room while she was trapped with Jacob, and her travel keyboard was right in the top. Fishing her tablet from her bag, she connected the two together, sat down and started to make notes. She'd change everything around, of course, but the experience was too unique, too special, not to find its way into her work somehow. *'Write what you know'* was always the best advice, after all!

*

Ellie hadn't expected the conference to be so busy. She'd managed to meet several of her favorite authors and sold far more books than she expected to. There was a constant flow of fans eager to meet her and have her autograph books for them; by the end of the first day her hand hurt from signing autographs and shaking hands, and her face felt stiff from smiling. Still, she was hardly going to complain, she thought to herself with a smile, tidying up the mess of books and promotional materials scattered all over her table.

The flow of customers had dried up to a trickle and she knew that the doors would be closing in the next few minutes; only the most popular authors still had a short line of people waiting to meet them. Soon she could head back to the hotel and order room service, put her feet up and maybe make some notes for her next book. She was way too nervous about being in New York City at night to go out to eat alone, even though her writer's soul mourned the loss of the experience.

A shadow fell across her as she leaned across the table to scoop up some stray bookmarks; Ellie plastered her smile back on again and looked up.

"You're not an easy woman to track down, *Barbie Belle*," Jacob said with a warm smile.

The bookmarks fell from Ellie's suddenly nerveless fingers. "I didn't think you'd bother," she gulped.

"Didn't you? I haven't been able to stop thinking about you."

"Really?" He looked gorgeous, she thought, in a tight white T-shirt that showed off the breadth of his shoulders, those sinfully tight blue jeans and the now-battered cowboy hat on his head.

"Really. I've been all over this place lookin' for you all day." He propped a hip on the table, picked up a book off one of the stacks. Ellie's face flamed as he looked at it, smirking at the book cover.

"This guy your usual type?" Jacob glanced up at her, tapping his thumb on the image of the long-haired, bare-chested Highland warrior wearing a kilt and brandishing a broadsword.

"It's my specialty. What I'm known for," she confessed. "Everyone loves a laird, as the saying goes."

"Mom reckons it's 'everyone loves a cowboy', actually." He grinned, white teeth flashing in his handsome face, the cowboy hat shading his beautiful blue eyes slightly. They still twinkled with a wicked light, the corners crinkling up as he smiled.

"I must admit to a certain new-found fondness for cowboys myself. Especially cowboys who are actually architects." Encouraged by his attention, Ellie lost a little of her nervousness and smiled back at him.

"That's good." Jacob reached out, curled a hand around her waist and lightly tugged, bringing her closer. "Because this fake cowboy-architect was hopin' that you might come out to dinner with him."

"You were?" She let him pull her close, right up against his body until her breasts were pressed against his chest.

"Sure. I know a great little Italian place not too far from here. Do you like Italian food?"

Food of any kind was the last thing on Ellie's mind at that moment as Jacob's hands warmed her skin through her blouse. She couldn't seem to pull her gaze away from his lips, sensuous and full. When she didn't speak, Jacob groaned softly.

"Y'all need to stop lookin' at my mouth like that, Ellie, or I'm gonna suggest we skip dinner and go straight to dessert."

"Dessert?" she said a bit numbly, stunned by the way he was looking at her.

"Yeah." Lowering his head to hers, he whispered "Cream. I didn't get to taste yesterday," before his lips slanted over hers in a slow, hungry kiss.

Ellie sagged against Jacob, her hands coming up to clutch at his shirt. Absorbed in the kiss, they both forgot where they were until a passer-by wolf-whistled at them. Jacob lifted his head unhurriedly, grinning down at Ellie.

"While I'm very tempted, I promised myself that I was gonna take you out." He lifted one hand, brushed a straggling strand of hair behind her ear gently. "And then later, I'm gonna take you *in*, in all the ways I can imagine. And I've got a very good imagination."

She shivered with desire as his eyes blazed at her, nodded mutely. Jacob dropped his hand from her waist, looked around the booth. "You finished here?"

"Almost." She shoved the rest of the books hastily into her storage box, stowed it under her table. Tidied her bookmarks into haphazard piles with shaking fingers, smoothed her wayward hair again before smiling nervously at Jacob. "There. That'll do until tomorrow."

"Good." He straightened up, reached for her hand, his long, warm fingers folding securely around hers. "You hungry?" he asked as he led her from the conference center.

"Starving," Ellie admitted. She'd been too busy to stop for lunch, and breakfast seemed like a very long time ago.

"Excellent." Jacob squeezed her hand, his glance down at her filled with filthy promise. "You're gonna need the energy."

Determined to give as good as she got, Ellie squeezed back. "So are you. I'm fully intending to live up to the theme of my favorite country song."

Jacob cocked an eyebrow at her curiously. "What's that?"

"Save a horse, ride a cowboy!" she grinned wickedly up at him, enjoying the way he laughed heartily at her joke.

"I'm looking forward to that *very* much!"

~   **The End**   ~

ELEVATOR ENCOUNTERS

Juliet's Romeo

"Welcome to the Westlake Hotel, Miss Stafford. We hope you enjoy your stay."

"Thank you." Juliet accepted the proffered key card envelope, glanced at the number on it. "912; the ninth floor?"

"That's correct, Miss Stafford." The desk clerk nodded. "The restaurant is located on the ground floor, through those doors there, and the hotel gym is on the fourth floor, should you wish to make use of it."

She nodded, accepting the information, and turned towards the elevators. There was a bank of three, the doors gorgeously patterned in an Art Deco kind of pattern which matched the hotel's age and overall décor. She punched the call button and stood waiting, her artist's eye absorbing the geometric patterns. She wanted to sketch it, and soon. Well, she'd have plenty of time; she was due to stay here for several weeks while working on the murals she'd been commissioned to refurbish in the hotel's dining room. She wondered if the doors were patterned the same way on every floor, or if she'd have to come back to the lobby to draw them.

There was a discreet *ping*, and the doors to the elevator on the far left side slid open. Juliet moved over to enter, pulling her wheeled case of art supplies with her. She'd left her suitcase with the porter to bring up shortly, but nobody touched her paints and brushes but her.

"Oh," she said in admiring surprise, gazing at the floor of the elevator; even the carpet fitted with the Art Deco theme. Juliet had never seen the pattern before, and it was clearly of recent make, plush and thick. Specially commissioned, she suspected. "Nice," she murmured aloud, before realizing that the elevator wasn't moving. Reaching out, she punched the button for the ninth floor — noting in passing that the brass buttons appeared to be original as well. Returning her gaze to the carpet, she didn't really pay attention to the passing seconds. When the doors slid open with another discreet *ping*, she stepped forward, still gazing at her feet — and collided heavily with a warm, solid body.

"Oh, I'm so sorry!" a deep voice said as she stumbled back, and two strong hands caught her by the waist, steadying her. "Are you all right?"

Blinking, Juliet looked up into a pair of very dark brown eyes, set in a craggily handsome face. A *familiar* face. She blinked again. "Uhm," she said vaguely, staring. "Uhm. You're Nico Romero."

"Guilty as charged, and I'm also the idiot who nearly mowed you down as you were trying to get out of the elevator. This your floor?" Nico smiled appreciatively down at the woman he'd almost trampled. She was tiny, which explained how he'd completely missed her when the elevator doors opened, barely five feet tall to his six foot three. She was also really gorgeous, with long silken dark brown hair cascading messily from a knot caught up on top of her head, eyes the color of freshly mown grass and a figure that most definitely caught his attention. He tried to keep his eyes on hers rather than letting them drop to the magnificent breasts pushing at her thin T-shirt.

The paint-splattered T-shirt. Maybe the paint splatters were an excuse to drop his eyes. *No, Nico, don't be an ass. Eyes up.*

"Uhm." Juliet dragged her star-struck gaze from the face of one of the biggest movie stars in the world, looked at the floor number. *Four.* "Oh. No. Sorry. My fault, I shouldn't have been getting out anyway."

"Not going to the gym?" She was kind of dressed for it, in the paint-stained old tee, leggings and running shoes.

"No, I just arrived." Juliet shook her head. "Going to my room. Ninth floor." *Talk in complete sentences, Juliet,* she chastised herself. *You sound like an idiot.*

"Sure." Nico removed the foot which had been preventing the doors from closing, reached across to punch the top button on the panel. The doors slid closed and the elevator started to move upwards again.

Juliet couldn't stop staring at Nico as he moved to lean against the opposite wall of the elevator, propping a hip against the brass handrail. He must have been in the gym working out, she realized; he had a towel draped over one shoulder, used it now to wipe at a light sheen of sweat on his face. Her eyes slid downwards, over the old T-shirt with the sleeves ripped out to reveal beautifully muscled arms. Down further, to take in the fact that he was wearing… *tight Lycra shorts?*

Okay, I think I must have fallen and hit my head, because quite clearly I'm imagining all of this. There is no way — NO WAY — that I am sharing an elevator with Nico Romero, megastar heartthrob, wearing Lycra shorts.

Just as she was telling herself that — and trying to pull her eyes away from the very sizable bulge in the shorts in question — the elevator shuddered and ground to a halt, the light dimming and flickering out, leaving only a small emergency light on over the control panel.

*

"What the hell?" Nico murmured when nothing happened after a moment. The number on the scrolling display appeared to be frozen between 7 and 8. He punched a couple of floor buttons, tried the Door Open. "I think it's broken down," he said, probably redundantly, turning to look at his companion. She stared back at him from wide grass-green eyes, said nothing.

"Um. Maybe I can get the doors open, see if we're actually at a floor…" but the doors stubbornly refused to yield when he sought to wedge his fingers in the crack.

Juliet stared, wondering if her eyes were actually going to pop out of her head, as muscles visibly rippled in Nico's back beneath his tight, sweat-dampened shirt and his ass tightened even further.

"Is that even legal?"

"What?" Nico turned to look at her. Realizing she'd spoken aloud, Juliet backtracked hastily.

"There's an emergency call button," she pointed at the control panel. "Better give that a try."

"Yeah, I guess." Turning back to the panel, Nico punched the button. A loud ringing sound was followed by a bored-sounding, tinny voice from the small speaker.

"Brooklyn Elevator Services; please could I get your elevator reference number?"

"Uh," Nico looked at the panel. A small hand reached past him, a fingertip tapping at a series of engraved letters and digits near the bottom. He read them off, glancing over at his companion with a grateful smile.

"Elevator Number Three at the Westlake Hotel, is that correct?" The voice sharpened slightly.

"That's right. At least, we're in one of the elevators at the Westlake…"

"And how many people are there in the elevator, sir?"

"Two," Nico glanced at the woman again. She'd folded her arms and was leaning back against the wall, looking resigned.

"I see. I've alerted the repair technician; he has advised that he is en route to your location but he is quite some distance across town. He may take up to an hour to get to you. Will that be all right?"

"I suppose it'll have to be," Nico said with a shrug.

"Please press the alarm button if you should need to speak to me again in the meantime," the voice said, before there was a click and the line went dead.

"Well," Nico said after a few moments of silence. "I guess we're stuck."

"Duh," Juliet said before she could stop herself, but Nico only grinned at her sarcasm.

"Yeah, you're right, I'm being Captain Obvious. Sorry. Nico Romero," he held a hand out in an offer to shake.

"It's Captain Frostbite, isn't it, not Captain Obvious?" Juliet said with a cheeky grin, unfolding her arms and accepting his hand.

"Ugh," Nico grimaced at the memory of one of his early roles. It had been an awful superhero movie; he'd since moved on to bigger and better things, including a more recent, and *much* more successful, comic-book adaptation he'd directed himself. "I prefer Shadow Commando, if you don't mind." He held onto her hand, feeling how delicate it felt in his, fine-boned and soft. "And you are…? Wait, I know. You must be the Rainbow Witch," he gestured at the multi-colored paint splatters on her shirt.

Juliet laughed at the clever comeback, but she also found herself blushing. The Rainbow Witch was the Shadow Commando's love interest in the movie, played by an absolutely stunning A-list actress. "Are they going to get together in the sequel?" she couldn't help but ask.

"That would be telling." Nico winked at her, smiled his famous quirky smile.

I am a grown woman, I am not going to swoon at his feet like a teenage fangirl…

"So if you're not the Rainbow Witch, who are you really?" Nico finally let go of her hand.

"Juliet," she said, still a bit stunned by his sheer charisma. "Juliet Stafford."

"But that's even better; Romero and Juliet!"

"Oh, stop it." She laughed helplessly. Nico grinned, happy to have put her at ease. He hadn't missed the star-struck look. Folding his long legs, he sank to sit down on the elevator floor, patted the plush carpet beside him.

"Might as well get comfortable. We're gonna be here a while. So what brings you to the Westlake, Juliet Stafford?"

"Work," she plucked at her T-shirt as she settled down to sit beside him. "I'm a painter; a restoration expert, actually. I've been hired to restore the murals in the dining room."

"Really?" Nico looked delighted. "I love those murals. They're the reason I always stay here in the Westlake whenever I'm in New York. I've always enjoyed the ones in the RCA building at Rockefeller Center, the Frank Brangwyn ones, but I actually like the ones here better. The colors are brighter."

"They are," Juliet nodded, impressed at his knowledge. "Unfortunately some of the pigments which were used to paint them are degrading — they're over eighty years old, after all — and the general grime of the city is starting to get to them. Hence, my job."

"That's really cool." Nico nodded approvingly. "I shall definitely come by and see how you are getting on."

She blushed a little, looked down at her hands. Trying to keep her eyes away from the long, leanly muscled thigh stretched out very close to hers. "What brings you to New York?" she asked curiously, doing her best to sound as though she was merely making polite conversation.

"We've got location shoots for *Shadow Commando 2* starting next week. I've been going around with the camera guys and the set dressers — I'm directing again, so everything needs to be perfect before I get the other actors on set." He gestured down at himself, offered her a self-deprecating grin. "And obviously, the role demands I be in pretty good shape."

"You look in pretty good shape to me," Juliet said dryly. It was a definite understatement; he looked as though there wasn't an ounce of fat on him, he was all solid muscle. She couldn't keep her eyes from tracing up those long, muscled thighs again. Those cycling shorts were probably indecent, but then, he hadn't been wandering around in public. He probably hadn't been expecting to see anyone on the way back to his room, much less run into a fan who couldn't keep her eyes off said thighs…

Nico shifted, re-adjusting his position, and Juliet dragged her eyes away, cheeks burning.

"You look kinda hot. You okay?" he asked solicitously.

*

"I'm fine!" Juliet almost squeaked it. "I mean, yeah, it's kind of warm in here," she seized gratefully on the excuse for her red cheeks.

"You want a drink?"

She hadn't noticed before, but he was carrying an insulated drink bottle, offered it to her now.

"Oh," she blinked at the proffered bottle, accepted it to take a sip. "What is it — water?"

"Lemon-lime sports drink."

She'd just discovered that for herself, made a small face. "Yark."

"Not a favorite?" Nico accepted the bottle back, grinning.

"I'm afraid not. Save it for if we really need it, huh? Like if we're stuck in here more than an hour."

He nodded and set the bottle aside. Leaned back against the wall of the elevator with a sigh, crossed his ankles and steepled his fingers together. Silence fell for a couple of minutes that felt like an eternity to Juliet. She shifted around awkwardly, wondering what on earth she could say. Surely being trapped in an enclosed space with Nico Romero was every girl's fantasy… she'd certainly entertained the thought a time or two. Even dreamed of him once or twice. Although in her dreams, there'd been a lot less silent staring and a lot more kissing and touching.

Licking her lips, she darted a glance at Nico and found, much to her surprise, that he was watching her. He snatched his gaze away quickly, then looked back at her and smiled a bit awkwardly.

"Sorry, I was staring."

"Why?" Juliet blurted, startled.

"Because you're gorgeous?" Nico looked surprised that she'd asked. "You have the most amazing bone structure." He reached out, traced a fingertip lightly along the arch of her brow, the curve of her cheekbone. "The camera would adore you."

She shook her head at once. "No. No way. I'm an artist, my place is behind the camera, not in front of it."

"Shame." He was still touching her face, traced his finger gently beneath her chin. "Your kind of beauty is uncommon these days. Everyone goes for the flashy looks, but you've got something different. You'll still be stunning when you're eighty, like Lauren Bacall."

"Oh," Juliet honestly didn't know what to say. Nobody had ever paid her such a high compliment, and she sensed that Nico was being completely honest. "I… I bet you say that to all the girls," she stuttered out finally.

Nico blinked, shook his head and laughed, dropping his hand from her face at last. "I can honestly say that I've never said that to another woman. Not ever."

Juliet stared at him for a moment in silence, judging the sincerity on his face. He was an actor, after all — but she was pretty sure she'd never seen that particular expression on his face on the big screen. On impulse, she leaned in and pressed her lips against his.

Nico looked absolutely astonished when she pulled back. "What was that for?"

"Come on," Juliet chucked at his expression. "That's never happened to you before? You're a movie star. You must get unwanted kisses planted on you all the time."

"I wouldn't call that one unwanted."

"I couldn't resist, when would I ever get the opportunity again… what?" She blinked.

"It wasn't an unwanted kiss." Nico shrugged, the famous dimple in his chin flashing as he smiled. "When will I ever get trapped in an elevator with a girl as beautiful as you again? It's like the beginning of a classic rom-com."

"I don't think I've seen that movie."

"I don't think anyone ever made that movie. Or if they did, it was a Hallmark made-for-TV one." His dimple flashed again, and Juliet started to laugh.

"You're making me want to look up elevator movies."

"All the ones I can think of are horror, so don't." Nico leaned over towards her, reached to touch her cheek again, stroking away a curl of hair which toppled in front of her eye. "Help me figure out what would happen next in the rom-com instead." His voice was low and husky.

"Well," Juliet licked her lips, "it's definitely a rom-com, is it?"

"It could be another kind of movie entirely," Nico murmured, leaning even closer. "The kind where an attraction between two people is just too intense to deny…"

Lips met in a slow, lingering kiss. Nico's breath was warm, the kiss light at first and then hotter, hungrier. He sucked Juliet's lower lip between his, nibbled at it gently. One heavily muscled arm slipped around her as she leaned in towards him.

Slender fingers crept tentatively up Nico's chest, brushed against his collarbone. He shuddered as the tip of her thumb brushed the hollow of his throat; he'd always been sensitive there. It was an extremely erogenous zone for him, and Juliet's light, tentative touch had just as powerful an effect as if she'd touched the tip of his cock. He moaned into her mouth, pulling her closer, a little startled when she came more than willingly, lifting a leg to straddle his lap. The tip of Juliet's thumb traced the hollow of his throat again and Nico tipped his head back with a desperately needy little sound.

*

Juliet was briefly surprised as Nico threw his head back, strong neck arching. He looked sexy as hell, especially with the small noise he made in his throat, and she couldn't resist leaning in to lick up that beautiful neck, taste the cords in his throat. He made the noise again, louder, his fingers biting in on her hips.

"You like that?" Juliet whispered, nibbling at his throat. Licking softly along his collarbone, her hands settling on his broad shoulders.

"Oh God, please don't stop," Nico gasped helplessly. "That feels so damn good!"

Even though he'd obviously been sweating during his workout, he tasted good, a clean, masculine tang of salt and musk that made her thirsty for more. She nibbled and suckled at his neck, surprised and gratified by his low moans of pleasure, the way his hips shifted against her. It was more than obvious that he was aroused, his erection a hard bar pushing against her through their clothes. Juliet found herself getting aroused too, grinding back against Nico, rubbing her breasts against his chest. Her nipples ached, desperate for stimulation — stimulation which Nico promptly offered as his hands came off her hips and up to cup her breasts, thumbing through the thin, aged fabric of her T-shirt and the silk of the bra she was wearing beneath.

Juliet made a frantic, wordless sound against Nico's throat, and suddenly he shifted under her, tipping her back off his lap, though one arm caught her before she hit the floor, eased her down to the soft carpet before he came down atop her, pausing with his face a couple inches above hers.

"If you don't want to do this, now would be a really good time to tell me to stop. Otherwise, I plan to spend the time until we get rescued exploring every inch of that delectable body of yours."

She still had the vague sensation that this was all some fantastic dream, that she couldn't really be here with Nico Romero with those famous big brown eyes gazing into hers.

But if it was a dream, it was the best one she'd ever had and she really, really didn't want it to stop any time soon.

"Shut up and kiss me again," she demanded.

*

Nico laughed delightedly as Juliet stared back up at him from those bright green eyes and, far from telling him to stop, *demanded* that to kiss her again.

"What a woman," he marveled softly, amazed that of all the people he could get trapped in an elevator with, it should happen to be this one; a feisty, beautiful and willing woman who pushed all of his buttons.

"Sh," she ordered, and her small hands came up, threaded into his hair, and yanked hard, pulling his mouth down on hers.

Her lips were soft and pillowy, her mouth sweet-tasting; Nico could have taken intense pleasure in just kissing her for hours, exploring that delicious mouth, but there were much more wonderful delights to investigate. Those bountiful breasts sized just perfectly to fit his big hands, for example.

Juliet was tugging at the back of his shirt; he reared back off her long enough to drag it over his head and throw it aside. Braced on his arms above her, he smiled at her expression. She was blatantly admiring the muscles of his chest and shoulders, the muscles he'd spent so many painful hours in the gym to hone.

He'd many times directed the cameras to dwell lovingly on his muscles, knowing very well that legions of fans would swoon over them when his movies screened. It was always an impersonal knowledge, though, and seeing Juliet's wide eyes, the way she licked her lips, suddenly made all those agonizing hours very much worth it.

Juliet lifted a hand to ghost it delicately over his chest, tracing lightly down between his pecs to investigate the perfect six-pack of his abs, delineating the muscles with the tips of her fingers wonderingly.

"Holy crap, I always thought these were like… highlighted with clever makeup. You know. Contouring."

Nico snort-laughed. "They are, for the camera."

"Yeah, but they're also completely real. Very, very real. Very. Um." She trailed her fingertips down the fine line of hair running down into the waistband of his shorts. "Ummm."

"My eyes are up here," he snickered at her distraction.

"Oh, like you weren't staring at my boobs before," she looked up to meet his eyes, grinning at his guilty look. "It's OK. Tit for tat. Or tits for abs, as is actually the case."

Once again, Nico found himself laughing, liking this lovely woman more and more with every word out of her mouth that demonstrated her down-to-earth attitude, her sense of humor. "Well, I've shown you mine," he teased. "Fair's fair."

Juliet smiled as he leaned back further. He was straddling her thighs, looking down at her; it could have been an intimidating pose, but his smile and the admiring warmth in his expression made her feel quite comfortable. Letting her hands drop from his abs reluctantly, she grabbed the hem of her T-shirt and tugged it upwards.

Nico reached down to help her pull the shirt off over her head; it promptly followed his into a dark corner of the elevator.

"Stunning," he breathed, looking at the white silk bra she was wearing underneath and the generous breasts filling the fabric cups, nipples pushing against the thin fabric making it obvious that she was nearly as aroused as he was. A soft blush spread up her chest, and she cast her eyes down a little shyly.

"Come on, you've filmed love scenes with some of the most beautiful women in Hollywood."

"Who are pretty much inevitably size zeros. With either the breasts that naturally come with being a size zero, or unnaturally inflated balloons. Give me a real woman any time, one with real curves." The tips of his fingers grazed down her sides, tracing the hourglass shape of breasts to waist and out to her hips. "And boy, have you got hella curves."

Charmed and seduced by his obvious appreciation of her assets, Juliet reached for his hands, catching them in hers and bringing them to her breasts. "Feel free to appreciate as much as you like," she suggested, shifting to twist an arm behind her back and unhook her bra.

Grinning with appreciation for her boldness, Nico was more than happy to remove her bra as it came away from her skin, drawing it up her arms and discarding it. "Beautiful," he hummed in appreciation, filling his hands with her generous breasts. "Absolutely stunning." Her nipples were peaked into hard little brown acorns, stiffening even further as he brushed his thumbs over them. Eager for a taste, he licked his lips, shifting backwards and leaning down to take one into his mouth.

Juliet moaned as Nico's hot mouth worked her nipple, his tongue flicking over it before he suckled it deep into his mouth. His large, strong hands were almost reverent as he touched her; Juliet couldn't remember any past lover's caresses being half so tender. Not that she was thinking about any of those past lovers now, not with Nico's powerful body pressing down on hers, his stubble a sensuous rasp on her skin as his mouth worshiped her breasts.

She must have made some sound, probably an embarrassing noise of ecstasy deep in her throat, because Nico lifted his head. His blue eyes twinkled with amusement as he asked "Am I crushing you?"

Juliet shook her head and reached for him, threading her hands into his hair and pulling his head back down to her breasts in a wordless demand to continue. Nico laughed quietly, but obeyed her silent command with alacrity.

*

Juliet lost track of how long they lay there, Nico suckling and kissing her breasts, moving from one to the other, squeezing them lightly in his big hands, his fingers working whichever nipple his mouth wasn't currently occupied with pleasuring. Heat arrowed through her body; she was sure that her pussy was bubbling with need, drenching her panties and probably soaking through to her leggings. Her nails scratched at Nico's scalp, drawing low sounds of pleasure from him. Finally he lifted his head, moving up over her to kiss her mouth.

"I want you," he said, voice even deeper and rougher than usual. "I want you so fucking bad, Juliet."

"Mm-hm," she agreed, a little dazed as he moved off her, mourning the loss of his body heat. He sat up and immediately pulled her into his lap, though.

"But we've already done more than is probably wise, considering that we could be interrupted any moment." Nico couldn't resist her, pressing slow, sucking kisses along her collarbone in between words, his hands inexorably drawn back to those magnificent breasts. "We really should stop."

"Don't wanna," Juliet mumbled sulkily, nails scraping down his muscled biceps as he squeezed her nipples gently in his fingertips.

"Me neither." He sought her mouth for another kiss, tongue dancing with hers in a teasing battle. "Want to strip the rest of your clothes off and make you scream my name." He ground his hips up at her, the rock-hard evidence of his arousal pushing at her through the thin layers of his shorts and her leggings. "But I gotta think of you. If we're caught and you get outed as the woman who Nico Romero was gettin' busy with in a hotel elevator…"

The very idea was like a dash of cold water in the face. Juliet sighed, buried her face against his neck. "Damn it, why do you have to be right?"

"Sorry, beautiful," he stroked her hair, nuzzling at her ear. "Don't think this is over, though. We started somethin' here, and I want to finish it, if you're willing. What's your room number?"

It had momentarily escaped her lust-fogged brain. Sighing, she scrambled off Nico's lap and reached for her purse, scrabbling for the key folder she'd been handed at reception. "912," she told Nico, reaching for her bra and shirt, tossing Nico's shirt back into his lap. Just in time, too, because as he pulled it over his head the elevator shook slightly before starting to descend.

Panicking, Juliet just yanked her own T-shirt on and shoved her bra into her purse. By the time the doors slid open, she was standing in the opposite corner of the elevator car to Nico, clutching her purse to her chest, her eyes wide, cheeks flushed, quite sure that the evidence of what they'd been up to was painted all over her face.

"Afternoon sir, miss," an elderly man wearing mechanic's overalls said as he stepped into the elevator. "Apologies for the breakdown. Number Three is a stubborn old girl."

Nico smiled, apparently amused, as the old man fondly patted the vintage brass control panel before removing a pair of screws and sliding out a fuse. "Sounds like it's been a long and stormy relationship."

"You could say that." The repairman chuckled, inserting a new fuse. "There we go, she should behave now. Let me make sure you get to your floors. Sir?"

"Sixteen. And nine for the lady." Nico nodded towards Juliet, who was still too embarrassed at almost having been caught *in flagrante delicto* to say a word. Thank goodness Nico had the sense to call a halt, she thought, because if it had been up to her they'd have been naked and fucking hard on the elevator floor when it started to move. She swallowed hard at the thought, unable to stop wondering how Nico might feel buried deep inside her.

"Ninth floor, miss," the repairman's voice broke her reverie.

"Oh. Yes, thank you." Grabbing the handle of her art case, she wheeled it out of the elevator. She couldn't quite meet Nico's eyes; the whole encounter was beginning to feel more unreal by the second.

Just as the doors slid closed, she heard Nico's deep voice say "It was nice to meet you, Juliet."

She turned too late to meet his eyes. Only the blank metal of the closed doors greeted her. Biting her lip, she shook her head and turned away to find her hotel room.

*

Finally reaching the sanctuary of her room, Juliet looked around briefly before flinging herself down on the bed. Absently, she noted that her suitcases were there already, presumably delivered by the porter while she was trapped in the elevator with Nico.

Trapped in an elevator with Nico Romero — she shook her head incredulously. Just meeting him was like something right out of a dream, never mind what had actually occurred in the elevator, what they had done. Pushing herself off the bed, she went into the bathroom, peered at herself in the mirror. Her eyes looked wide and shocked, her lips kiss-swollen — and she definitely didn't have a bra on underneath her T-shirt.

"It really did happen," Juliet said to her reflection, pulling down the neck of her T-shirt to inspect the blooming hickey on her collarbone. After several long moments of staring at herself, she finally shook her head and turned to switch on the shower.

The torrent of hot water pouring over her did little to dispel the feeling of unreality that still permeated her brain. Sighing, Juliet took her time in the shower, luxuriating in the endless stream of hot water. Her own shower in her tiny apartment hardly compared; the hotel offering her complimentary room and board while she worked on restoring the murals had been an unexpected bonus she'd have been silly to turn down, especially since she'd been able to sublet her apartment to a friend of a friend temporarily.

She was wrapped in one of the hotel's complimentary bathrobes, toweling her hair dry with the thickest, fluffiest towel she'd ever held, when there was a knock on the door.

Startled, Juliet froze. That couldn't be… *no. No, he wouldn't…*

She had to stand on her tiptoes to peer through the peephole, muttering to herself about builders who didn't consider short people. The mutters died into silence as she saw the handsome visage of Nico Romero outside her door.

Juliet dropped down to her heels before toeing back up again for a second look. Yes, he was still standing there, a hopeful little smile on his face.

She couldn't just leave him standing there, no matter how shocked she felt. Her hand closed on the door handle and she swung the door wide.

"Hi," Nico said with a broad smile. The smile faded, his expression turning a little quizzical as he took in the bathrobe bundling her up, the towel dangling from one hand, her wet hair. "Uh. Oh. You weren't expecting me. I should… I should go."

"No. No, don't go," Juliet said quickly, clutching onto the door handle for support. "Err… come in. You can't stand in the hallway, someone might see you…"

He smiled a little crookedly as he stepped forward into the room and she closed the door behind him. "Nico Romero caught sneaking into mystery beauty's hotel room!"

"Yeah, not a headline I'd like to be the *mystery* part of." She smiled up at him, put at ease by his joking tone, the way he put his hands in his pockets and moved away to give her space, walking over to the window to look out at the view.

"Nice room. The hotel comped you?" Nico glanced over his shoulder at her, still standing uncertainly by the door.

"Yes… but you already knew that, huh?" She cocked an eyebrow at him.

His smile was a little sheepish. "My security detail were understandably a little stressed out when I got back to my suite. I had to give them something to do."

"So you set them to checking me out." She couldn't be mad with him, not really. It was only natural for someone as in the public eye as Nico, to be wary about the people he was associating with. She, however, had absolutely nothing to hide.

"You checked out, of course," he confirmed her suspicion. "But… I think I'd still have come even if they *had* turned up something hinky on you."

"Would you?" Finally she moved away from the door, throwing the wet towel in her hand through the bathroom door as she passed it. "I have to admit I didn't really think you would."

"Why?"

It was a simple, direct question, and Juliet considered it thoughtfully before giving him honesty in return. "Because for a good few minutes there I was convinced I was imagining things. That I'd had a really vivid hallucination or something, because there's just no way that I got trapped with Nico Romero in an elevator and…"

"And," he agreed with a grin as she tailed off. "It's the *and* part that's why I'm here, of course."

"Yes," she nodded, a little breathless as he moved away from the window and walked toward her slowly.

"Because there could be quite a lot more. We started something in that elevator, Juliet, and I'd like to see where it goes. If that's something you'd be interested in."

He too had showered; this close she could smell the clean, fresh scent rising from his skin, woodsy and masculine. He'd been gorgeous in his sweaty gym clothes; in chinos and a dark blue Henley the only word she could find to describe him was *breathtaking*.

"I would… I would be interested," Juliet confirmed breathlessly.

"If you'd like to take it slow I'd be good with that. We could maybe get dinner together or something — though room service would probably be the best policy because I tend to get mobbed at restaurants unless I reserve a private room…"

She could only imagine. Shaking her head, she smiled. "Thanks for the offer, though. Room service sounds good." Biting down on her lower lip and taking a deep breath to gather her courage, she said

"But it's rather early for dinner. I'm not hungry yet. Maybe… you could help me work up an appetite?"

Nico's gaze followed her hands as she slowly untied the belt of her robe and let it fall open.

*

Juliet was entirely nude beneath the robe. Shrugging it off her shoulders and letting it fall to the floor, she smiled rather shyly at Nico, hoping he wouldn't think less of her for the bold action. His expression as he gazed back at her was near-reverent, though, making her feel more confident. Beckoning to him with one finger, she cast him a sultry smile and moved towards the bed.

"Fuck, Juliet," Nico said hoarsely, finally recovering from his frozen shock and starting after her. She sat down on the bed, swiveling to lift her legs up and reclining against the pillows, smiling up at him, arms open in welcome. "You sure?"

"Most definitely. I think I'd always regret it if I passed up the opportunity." Of course, she'd never talk about it to anyone, no matter what. She was a very private person, not the type to kiss and tell; she hoped he'd surmised that when he looked over the dossier his security had undoubtedly compiled on her.

Nico didn't hesitate any further; kicking off his shoes, he dragged his shirt off over his head and flung it aside, his blue eyes hot as he reached for her. "So fucking beautiful," he muttered, just before his lips closed again over one pouting nipple.

She hadn't imagined how good his mouth felt, how he used his hot tongue to press her nipple hard against the roof of his mouth and apply strong, sucking pressure. His warm hand curved around her breast at first, plumping and shaping, but the temptation for more was too strong with her lying there alongside him nude and inviting. His hand moved slow but sure, sliding down over her stomach to cup over her mound, long fingers delving into her cleft.

Nico made a pleased sound around his mouthful of flesh as he discovered how wet Juliet already was, slick juices greeting his exploring fingertips. She gave a soft little mewl as he grazed over her clit lightly, pushing down lower to slide two fingers right into her wet channel. He was only gathering moisture, though, almost immediately moved them back to scissor over her clit again, even as he suckled harder at her nipple.

"Oh fuck," Juliet panted. "Fuck, fuck!" She dug her short fingernails into Nico's shoulders, desperately seeking some sort of anchor against the overwhelming sensations his touch invoked. He gave her no respite, though, his fingers working faster, teeth joining his tongue to work her nipple just up to the edge of pain. Feeling her legs beginning to shake, the prickly warmth crawling up her spine, she gave in and succumbed, fireworks bursting behind her closed eyelids as she shuddered with climax.

"That's it," Nico finally let her nipple out of his mouth, pressed slow kisses all over her breast, his fingers gentling their strokes. "Damn, you're beautiful when you come," he marveled, watching Juliet's body arch with tension, her full lips parted, her breath coming in short pants. "Glorious." He didn't strop stroking gently over her clit, not until she reached down to push at his wrist. "Too much?"

"Too sensitive," she agreed breathily, eyes still closed. "Gimme a minute."

"Sure."

"And then I'm gonna return the favor, so get those pants off."

Nico chuckled, but he was far from averse to the idea. Rolling to his back briefly, he unfastened his belt and fly, shoved his chinos down and kicked out of them along with his shoes, before realizing that he should get the condoms he'd tucked hopefully into one of his pockets. He was wrestling them out, cursing his decision to button the pocket closed, when Juliet's slim hand closed over his cock, stealing his ability to think and breathe in one fell swoop.

"Do you usually go commando?" she asked, watching as the pants fell from Nico's slack grip, the condom box falling to the bed. He was generously sized, thick in her hand, rock-hard already with a little drop of precum showing at the tip. She swiped her thumb over it, stroking it into the silken, tight-stretched skin before beginning to work him in earnest.

"N-no," he stuttered, eyes drifting closed as her grip tightened and she stroked down towards the base of his cock and back up again, adding a twist as she reached the tip. "Ohhhh. Fuh. Nnn."

The fact that she could apparently make Nico Romero lose the ability for coherent speech was quite a gratifying feeling. Juliet watched his face as he fell back against the pillows, saw his lips part and his tongue lick at them convulsively, listened to his low groan of pleasure.

"Good?" she queried, snuggling in close to his side, laying her cheek against his chest.

"Unnnhhhh," he agreed in a wordless moan. She chuckled and sped up her strokes, working his cock harder and faster until his big hand settled on hers.

"Stop, angel."

She looked up at him with a pout, at least until he leaned over and kissed her long and slow.

"Don't think that I'm not enjoying it because I really, really am," Nico pulled his head back to say, "but keep that up and this is all gonna be over in a rather different manner than I hoped." Letting go of her hand, he picked up the forgotten condom box, raising his eyebrows in a silent question.

"Oh, well, when you put it that way." Juliet reached for the box and he let her take it, watching as she extracted a foil packet. "Let's get you dressed."

Nico lay back and tried to relax as Juliet rolled the condom on, though the teasing strokes and squeezes she gave were definitely not strictly necessary for the job at hand. The feel of her light, clever artist's fingertips teasing over his swollen, aching balls was almost too much to take. He fisted his hands in the sheet beneath him, unbearably tempted to roll her to her back, yank her ankles into the air and pound his cock brutally into her pussy until she screamed his name.

Without knowing if she would even enjoy that, though, he made himself say "Come ride me."

Juliet looked a little surprised, but moved willingly enough, swinging a leg over to straddle his hips. Her small size would make it awkward for her to sit astride him comfortably, he suspected, so he grabbed a couple of pillows to tuck under her knees.

"That's it," he murmured as she positioned herself, one slim hand wrapping around his cock, her hips rocking back and forth to rub the tip over her clit a few times before guiding it into the wet, heated cavern of her pussy. "Oh, damn, that feels so good, angel."

Juliet's dark brown hair was loose, tumbling over her shoulders, almost reaching her nipples, the wet strands sticking to her skin. He thought she looked beautiful, a sensual goddess taking her pleasure from his body. She threw her head back with a moan of pleasure as she sank slowly down on Nico's cock, her breasts jutting out in an open invitation he wasn't about to ignore. He reached up eagerly to fill his hands, squeezing and tugging at her nipples as she began to rock back and forth.

*

Nico's cock felt amazing plunged deep inside her; Juliet closed her eyes and leaned back, letting the sensations wash over her. His strong hands teased and plucked at her breasts, his hips shifting, pushing up towards her, encouraging her to move.

"Come on, angel," he exhorted her softly. "Come on, ride me, take what you want."

It felt wonderful, his cock stretching her wide open, pressing on all the sensitive spots inside her, but she needed friction. Flexing her thigh muscles, she lifted and lowered herself, but she couldn't settle to a rhythm. He was too big, his penetration too deep, and the bed had no headboard for her to hold on to for leverage. She sobbed in frustration.

"Nico, please!"

He groaned deep in his chest before dropping his hands from her breasts to grasp her hips. "What do you want, Juliet?"

"Want you to fuck me! Please! Please, I… I like it hard, rough…"

The sound he let out this time was more akin to a growl, blue eyes glinting hungrily as he easily reversed their positions, lifting her off him and flipping her to her back, moving quickly over her to kneel between her thighs. "Sounds good to me." He reached down to grasp one slim ankle, pulled it up to rest on his shoulder. "This work for you?"

"Oh god yes," she flung her hands up behind her, braced them on the wall behind the bed.

"Like this?" He didn't bother being gentle, pretty sure that what she wanted was the exact same thing he did. Lining up with her pussy, he slammed home with one quick thrust.

"Yes. Yes, Nico, yes, oh fuck yes, faster!" Her voice grew breathy and shrill, until she was almost shrieking as he began to move, setting up a fast, deep rhythm.

"Yeah?" he added a sharp twist of his hips on the next deep plunge, watching her green eyes glaze over with pleasure. "You like it hard, huh? Like a nice deep rough fucking?"

Juliet cried out his name, her dark hair thrashing on the white pillow as she flung her head from side to side. In the throes of her passion, she was the most sensual, erotic woman Nico had ever seen. His fingers clenched on her hips, holding her still for his rough, deep plunges inside her. She shrieked, uninhibited in her pleasure.

"Fucking glorious," Nico rasped out, gazing his fill as he thrust, taking his pleasure in Juliet's body and giving her plenty in return. Determined that she was going to come again, he took one hand off her hip and pressed his palm down on her stomach, thumb and forefinger working rapidly over her clit. Her cries redoubled, her heel digging into his shoulder as she strained against him, body bowing, her hips pushing up against him.

"More, Nico, please!" she begged him in a despairing scream, and he groaned, feeling sweat break out on his back. He'd known when he came down to her room that he would struggle to hold out for long; he'd wanted Juliet the first moment he laid eyes on her and discovering the depths of her passion only increased his lust. He could feel his climax like an onrushing train, unstoppable and inevitable. He only wanted to hold out long enough for her to come with him.

"Come on, angel," he exhorted, thumb working faster as his hips snapped back and forth. "Come on, let me feel you…"

She screamed, high-pitched and wordless, and he cried out himself as silken muscles clenched around him, milking his orgasm from him with an inevitable, inexorable pull.

Nico's groin ground against hers as he pressed himself deep, savoring every moment of her climax, of her body sucking greedily at his spurting, sensitive cock. Soft gasps and moans came from Juliet as she quivered beneath him; he stroked his hand gently down her stomach before carefully lowering her leg from his shoulder to the mattress and easing back, going to pull out.

"No," she reached for him, grabbed onto his forearm. "Not yet. Please. I — I like your weight on me, like feeling you in me."

He hesitated, wondering if he would crush her, before gingerly lowering himself to rest on his elbows. Her plump breasts pressed against his chest, her arms wrapping around his neck, and she sighed happily.

"Mm. So nice."

It *was* really nice, a closeness that he hadn't felt in a long time, literally just snuggling with another human being. It felt so good that when he heard her breathing begin to become a little labored with effort, he rolled to his back, slipping out of her but taking her with him to continue cuddling.

Juliet sighed contentedly, nestling her head into the crook of Nico's strong neck, listening to his slow, steady breathing. He stroked her hair gently, long slow passes of his hand over the damp silken strands.

It was a long time before either of them spoke. Juliet was beginning to feel a little awkward, wondering if Nico would just leave, or if she should ask him to stay. How long he was staying at the hotel. If he might be interested in seeing her again.

"So," Nico broke the silence at last, "about that dinner."

She smiled against his chest. "Room service? Or, I'm sure there are plenty of restaurants around here that deliver."

Nico smiled too, relieved. He'd been wondering if she wanted him to leave, and he was extremely reluctant to do that. "Sounds great. I've worked up an appetite."

Juliet giggled at that, looking up at him bright-eyed. "Me too," she traced a fingernail gently over his chest, circling slowly around one flat male nipple. Felt, to her surprise, Nico's cock twitch against her thigh.

"Keep doing that and you'll be starved by the time we get to order dinner," he said huskily, eyes locked with hers.

Juliet pretended to consider. "Well… you know, it'll take them a while to cook and deliver. Any ideas to fill in the time?"

Nico grinned with anticipation. "Oh, yeah, I can think of something. Why don't you find the menu while I go clean up? Then we can order and I can get you all dirty again."

She laughed delightedly, watching with appreciation as he headed for the bathroom before shaking her head at herself and getting up to look for the room service menu. She was absolutely *starving*.

*

Juliet winced as she climbed up another step on her stepladder. Her thighs were definitely letting her know about the unaccustomed exertion she'd indulged in the night before. She smiled as she thought of it; she and Nico had made love again while they waited for the food to be delivered, and then once more after eating, before Nico regretfully said he had to go. He had a late-night Skype call scheduled with a producer from his movie studio who was currently on a shoot in Australia.

"I wish I didn't have to go," he kissed the small of her back, where she lay sprawled and limp with pleasure, face-down in the middle of the bed, "but frankly, you've worn me out anyway."

"*I've* worn *you* out," she raised enough energy for a chuckle. "I don't think so."

Nico laughed too, pressed another regretful kiss on her spine. "Can I see you tomorrow?"

She was already drifting towards sleep. "Sure," she mumbled, thinking even in her punch-drunk state that he wouldn't bother. He'd had what he wanted, after all. And she, Juliet Stafford, had the memories of a night of passion with Nico Romero, one of the biggest movie stars in the world, to keep for a lifetime.

*

Juliet smiled as she used a solvent-soaked cotton swab to clean a patch of grime from a detail on one of the murals. And what memories they were; she'd never had a lover like Nico, fiercely passionate and yet considerate, careful of her smaller, weaker form even as he used his strength and power to fuck her harder she'd ever been fucked before.

She moved another step higher, groaning quietly as her thighs protested. She'd worked long hours today, she should probably quit soon and go find something to eat. She'd skipped lunch. Just a few more minutes. She'd almost finished cleaning this top corner…

"What a view," a deep voice said behind her, and she startled, looking around to see Nico looking, not at the murals, but at her ass.

Surprised, Juliet nevertheless grinned down at him. "You're supposed to be admiring the murals."

"Lovely, but they don't compare to the beauties of mother nature." He held up his arms. "Gonna come on down from there?"

"Got a good reason why I should?" she riposted.

Nico pretended to consider. "Dinner?"

"Room service again?"

"Was it so bad last time?" There was an appeal in Nico's blue eyes as he stared up at her that she found quite irresistible.

"Oh, it was tolerable, I suppose." She found it hard to keep a straight face as she descended the stepladder, gave up and burst out laughing as he grabbed her two rungs from the floor and swung her into his arms.

"Tolerable!" Nico exclaimed. "I'm insulted! I insist that you give me a chance to improve your assessment!" He was laughing too, and Juliet wound her arms around his neck, feeling suddenly very happy.

"I could be convinced."

He took her lips in a fiercely passionate kiss, tongue thrusting roughly into her mouth in a demonstration of exactly what he intended to do to her body shortly. Juliet moaned into his mouth, her arms tightening around his neck.

"Convincing enough?" Nico asked raggedly when he finally ended the kiss. Her lips swollen, eyes heavy-lidded with passion, Juliet smiled up at him.

"Let's go. Only," as he set her on her feet, "can we make sure not to take elevator number three this time? Because if we get stuck again, I really don't think I'll be able to restrain myself from ravishing you in it this time."

Nico's laughter trailed behind them as they left the room hand-in-hand. "You and me both, sweetheart!"

~   **The End**   ~

The Best Man For Leah

Leah kept her smile in place as she lowered her camera for the final time. "All done!"

The beautiful bride laughed happily. "Thank you so much, Leah, you've made this day perfect for us!"

"Well, I've tried, Heather." Leah accepted Heather's exuberant kisses on her cheeks. "Go on, now, Salvador is waiting for you. You don't want to miss your flight. Hawaii awaits!" She gestured to where Heather's new husband stood a few feet away, smiling indulgently as his wife hugged her best friend. "Have a few strawberry daiquiris on the beach for me, alright?"

"At least one a day!" Heather promised, and she was off in a rush of white skirts and joyous laughter, the happiest bride Leah had ever seen. She smiled, clipping the lens cap back onto her camera. Convincing Heather that being both the wedding photographer and the maid of honor would be impossible had taken some doing, but it meant Heather's sister had been forced to step in and actually do some of the work which would have otherwise all fallen on Leah's shoulders. It also meant she wasn't obliged to return to the party still going strong in the hotel's ballroom; she could just go upstairs to her room and crash out.

She debated going via the hotel bar and getting a drink to take upstairs with her, but then thought *what the hell*. She'd just pay the exorbitant rate for a bottle of wine from the mini bar. She could certainly afford it; though she'd offered to do the wedding photos for free, and Heather would probably have taken her up on it, Heather's new husband was absolutely loaded and had insisted on paying an extremely good price… in advance.

Smiling as she thought of her healthy bank account, Leah shouldered her camera bag and headed for the elevators. She punched the 'up' button and was waiting patiently for an elevator to arrive when a tall shadow loomed over her.

"Good evening," a deep, male voice said.

Leah knew that voice. She closed her eyes, praying briefly for patience. Salvador's even-better-looking but much-less-charming older brother, Sebastian Padilla, had been a thorn in her side ever since they'd met at the wedding rehearsal five days ago. He was a perfectionist, and literally nothing she and Heather had so painstakingly organized had been good enough in his eyes for his only brother's wedding. Heather had almost called the whole thing off in hysterics more than once; only Leah getting in Sebastian's face and shouting herself hoarse had finally silenced him. He was a Best-Man-Zilla.

She almost giggled as the irreverent thought popped into her head. Aloud, she said, "Mr Padilla," hoping her voice wouldn't quiver with the laughter she was trying to suppress. He probably wouldn't take being laughed at very well. She had to admit that she'd been very disappointed when she finally met Sebastian; Salvador had talked so often about how great his older brother was, what a wonderful sense of humor Sebastian had. Leah hadn't seen any evidence the man even knew how to laugh.

"Oh, I was hoping that we were past such formalities now, Leah," Sebastian said silkily. "After all, we're almost family. You and Heather are as close as sisters, and she's now married to my brother."

No thanks to you, Leah barely managed to bite back. She offered a polite smile anyway, thinking it was a good thing that Sebastian Padilla and she were unlikely to cross paths on a regular basis. She hardly moved in the same social circles as he did, and they wouldn't be meeting through Salvador and Heather too often, since the newlyweds were relocating to Chicago in a few weeks when Salvador took over a branch of the gigantic Padilla business empire there.

Thankfully, the elevator finally arrived, saving her from having to answer Sebastian. She stepped inside, turned to look for the control panel, but he was already in front of it.

"What floor?"

"Six," she answered, watched him punch the number as well as the one for the top floor. Of course. He was probably staying in the hotel's most expensive suite. Her eyes tracked down from the back of his smooth dark head, over his broad shoulders in his perfectly tailored suit. Not just designer, she thought, but bespoke, and damn did he fill it out well. Sebastian really fit the stereotype of the gorgeous asshole millionaire. Until he turned around to face her, gave her a friendly smile, and offered her an already-open bottle of champagne.

"What's that for?" Leah couldn't keep the surprise from her voice.

"Just thought you might like some." Sebastian shrugged. "I didn't purloin any glasses, I'm afraid, figured I'd find one in my room, but I thought you might like a drink."

She was tempted, but shook her head. "Didn't peg you as the type to swipe a bottle of champagne from the party and head to your room to drink alone. Or are you expecting company?"

"You offering to provide it?" Sebastian arched a black brow, smirking at her. His eyes raked her up and down, examining again the form-fitting designer knockoff dress she'd splurged a good chunk of her meagre savings on. No doubt it looked cheap to his gaze, accustomed as he would be to more refined offerings.

Leah was just opening her mouth to snap a denial at him when the elevator suddenly shuddered to a halt, the lights flickering and going out briefly before a small emergency light began to glow.

*

"What the hell was that?" Leah found herself clutching at the polished brass handrail, jolted back against the wall by the sudden stop.

"Elevator breakdown, I think." Sebastian pushed a couple of buttons on the control panel, attempted to force the doors, and swore under his breath. "Do you have your phone with you?"

"No, this is a wedding! I left it in my room. What about you, I thought you were surgically attached to that thing?" He'd certainly spent most of the last few days with his eyes glued to the screen.

"Well, in honor of my brother's wedding, I decided to leave mine in my room too. Which leaves us in a bit of a bind, doesn't it?"

Leah rolled her eyes, leaned past him, and jabbed the emergency button. "Pretty sure this'll be helpful."

A bored voice sounded tinnily from the little speaker on the panel, asking them their location and their problem. Sebastian gave the requested information.

"It's almost midnight, it may take a while for a repair person to get to you," they were told. "I'll send out an alert and then advise their ETA."

They waited in silence while they were put on hold, and then the operator came back on the line and told them the repair person should be with them in about an hour and a half. "Will you be all right until then?"

"I don't suppose we've got a lot of choice," Leah muttered under her breath. Of all the people to get stuck in an elevator with! Sighing as Sebastian thanked the operator, she decided she might as well get comfortable. Toeing out of her high heeled pumps, she slid down the wall to sit on the elevator floor, careless of what damage she might do to her dress. Her feet hurt too much for her to care.

"What are you doing?" Sebastian stared down at her. The operator had hung up, and it was very quiet in the elevator.

"Getting comfortable. I've been standing on these shoes all day and my feet have had quite enough, thank you." Leaning her head back against the antique timber paneling that lined the lower part of the elevator, she closed her eyes.

He was silent for a moment. She felt the elevator move very slightly as he sat down on the floor too, and then her eyes flew open as his hands curled around her ankles and he lifted her feet into his lap.

"What are you doing?" she squeaked as strong fingers began to firmly massage her insoles.

"It's not just today you've been on your feet the whole time. I'm not sure I've seen you sit down since we met, and you're always wearing heels. It can't be good for your feet."

"I'm only five-foot-two," Leah grumped. She debated snatching her feet away, but he really knew what he was doing with his hands. His thumbs dug firmly into the pads of her feet and she barely suppressed a groan. "I gotta wear heels or nobody takes me seriously."

"I take you seriously."

He *had* taken her seriously, Leah thought, leaning her head back and closing her eyes again. They'd clashed but he'd never once been dismissive of her. There had always been reasoning behind every dispute; not always reasoning she *agreed* with, but there had never been any element of 'because I say so' or 'because I know better than you'. He might be a bossy asshole but he'd always listened to what she had to say. And when she'd finally lost her temper, got in his face and told him to stop interfering because Heather was on the verge of calling the whole thing off, he'd at least had the common decency to shut up and butt out.

Sebastian let go of her right foot in favor of concentrating solely on her left, massaging her ankle firmly before working down and over her heel and instep again.

"Oh God, you're good at that." Leah had to speak or she'd make an embarrassing noise. "Thank you."

"You're welcome. I think you earned a foot massage or two. Thank you."

"For what?" She opened her eyes again, peering at him suspiciously.

"For going above and beyond to make Heather's — and by extension my brother's —

wedding day everything they could possibly have wanted. You did an incredible job."

She was so shocked that she gaped at him. Sebastian cocked a wry brow at her. "What?"

"You didn't seem to think so a couple of days ago when you were trying to call in an army of PAs and wedding planners to take over!"

"Leah…" He stared at her, a frown marring his handsome features. "Is that what you thought I was doing? I thought you were taking on too much, exhausting yourself. I saw you gulping down Advil dry before the rehearsal, figured the stress was getting to you. I just wanted to help."

Speechless with surprise, she stared at him. Sebastian sighed, resuming his massage of her feet. "I realized I was going about things all wrong when you blew up at me. Figured I'd best just shut my mouth because I was adding to your burden. I was wrong to doubt you; you had it all under control."

"I… I don't quite know what to say," Leah confessed after a moment of breathless silence. "I… really thought you were just a bossy asshole who wanted everything your own way."

Sebastian threw his head back and roared with laughter. Leah found herself giggling as well, relaxing for the first time in days, the laughter letting out the tension that had built up over the hectic weeks leading up to the wedding.

"I'm sorry," she managed to apologize between her giggles.

"No, no." Sebastian finally managed to quiet his own chuckles, shaking his head at her. "You're not wrong. I am a bossy asshole who's used to getting his own way, but you… I could see immediately that you were both competent and confident in your own ability. I honestly thought you were overloaded."

Impulsively, Leah leaned forward, putting her hand on his arm. "Thank you. I'm sorry I was too insecure to see that you were offering help. I just wanted everything to be perfect for Heather, and she… well, she's been my only family since I was seventeen and her folks took me in when I couldn't take living with my dad and stepmom any more."

"I understand." Sebastian took one hand off her foot, laid it over her fingers on his arm, and squeezed gently. "Sal is my baby brother, and the only family I have left, too. That's why I'm so grateful you worked so incredibly hard to make today perfect. I've never seen him so happy."

She smiled warmly at him, and he smiled back before taking his fingers off her arm, picking up the champagne bottle he'd set down on the floor of the elevator and offering it again.

"Drink?"

"Why the hell not." This time, Leah accepted. The heavy bottle was awkward to drink from, but it was nearly full so she didn't have to tip it up too far to take a sip. "I've never drunk champagne straight from the bottle before. How decadent." She handed it to Sebastian, who took a longer sip himself and grinned at her.

"Decadent can be fun."

"I wouldn't know."

"What, don't you ever let your hair down, Leah?" He looked at the smooth French roll she'd tamed her long red-brown hair into. "I bet you'd look stunning with it down."

Her name on his lips should not be making her stomach tighten into a quivering little ball. And that low, husky note in his voice should be illegal. Leah found her breath coming short.

"Is it hot in here?"

Oh my God, did I really just say that out loud?

Sebastian's smile was slow and knowing as he held her gaze. "I'm feeling quite warm," he agreed, and to her horrified fascination he leaned forward to slip his arms out of his jacket sleeves, discarding it to one side. His tie followed, and then he unfastened the top button of his shirt. The second. The third…

"Oh, don't stop there," Leah said impulsively as Sebastian's hands slowed.

He looked startled at her suggestive remark, his eyes and his grin both widening. "How much of that champagne have you had?"

"One sip! I stayed sober all night because I was taking photographs!" she said indignantly. "Speaking of which, stop hogging that bottle."

Sebastian handed it back, but he didn't return to unbuttoning his shirt, which was definitely a pity, Leah thought as she took another gulp of the champagne. It was really good champagne, as it should be at over a hundred bucks a bottle! Letting Sebastian select the champagne and other wines that had been served at the dinner was one of the few concessions she'd made, but then a multi-millionaire business owner *should* have much better taste in wine than a photographer who lived in a minuscule walk-up in Greenwich Village. Besides, he was paying for it. He'd paid for everything, refusing to let Salvador and Heather spend a cent.

Sebastian returned to massaging her feet, slow and sensual, really taking his time with the task. Leah failed to suppress the moan that welled up in the back of her throat as he rubbed the pads of his thumbs in slow, firm circles over the balls of her big toes. Embarrassed, she took another gulp of champagne, hoping against hope that he wouldn't say anything.

"I've been dreaming about you making those kind of noises, but I admit I imagined in it a slightly different scenario."

Leah choked and almost snorted champagne out of her nose. The coughing fit which followed was decidedly unsexy, but when she finally managed to stop, mopping at her streaming eyes, to her enormous surprise Sebastian wasn't laughing his ass off at her complete dorkiness. He was smiling slightly, carrying on with his sensuous rubbing of her feet.

"I really must be losing my touch. Normally women I'm attracted to know all about it pretty quickly."

"*You* are attracted to *me*? Why?" She had to be utterly unlike the women he normally encountered, high-powered, wealthy, put-together.

"I told you: you're confident and competent. Put those two qualities together in a beautiful woman and there's no way I can resist."

"I'm not beautiful." She said it firmly, shaking her head. She knew what she saw in the mirror every day. A snub nose, an over-wide mouth and skin so thickly freckled she'd need to apply makeup with a trowel to cover them all; most of the time she didn't bother. Eyes the color of a murky pond and a figure that was far too rounded to be fashionable.

"You're gorgeous." Sebastian said it with certainty, as though there was absolutely no doubt that he was correct.

"But you must get tall, skinny model types throwing themselves at you all the time!" She was no paparazzi, but as a photographer she'd done a bit of freelancing at society events, not to mention a few high-end weddings. She knew the world he moved in, and the type of women who frequented those events.

He shrugged. "Quite frequently, but they aren't my type. I like women with curves." His golden-brown gaze slid from her eyes down to her breasts and stayed there. "Real curves." His low voice dropped further, developing a husky rasp that would have melted her knees if she'd been standing up.

Leah gaped at him in pure astonishment. "Are you *flirting* with me?"

"Is it working?" Sebastian looked back up to her eyes, quirking a smile which revealed a surprising dimple in his cheek. "Yes, Leah, I'm flirting with you. Making a pass at you, expressing my interest… whatever you want to call it. Though hitting on you sounds a little crass, and I was trying to avoid that by waiting until after the wedding was over. Didn't want to create any awkwardness for Heather and Sal if you turned me down."

"Somehow, I get the impression you don't get turned down very often," Leah said drily.

Sebastian shrugged. "Not often. I rarely have to do the chasing, to be honest."

"I bet." He was blessed, after all, with the holy trifecta: money, good looks, and charm. She bet there were women throwing themselves at him on a daily basis. Hell, she'd witnessed several of the wedding guests doing just that. One or two of them had even been attending the wedding with their partners! "And yet, you're flirting with *me*."

"Didn't I tell you? You're confident, competent and gorgeous. How could I resist?" He was massaging her ankles again, long tanned fingers working slowly up her calves, pressing firmly into the tight muscles. It was dim in the faint glow from the elevator's emergency lighting but she could see his amber eyes locked onto hers, his expression openly admiring.

"Leah the Irresistible." She had to laugh at the thought, taking another swig of champagne and feeling suddenly reckless. "What are you waiting for, then? Stop resisting."

Sebastian's hands stilled. "I think you've had quite enough of that," he said finally, reaching out to take the bottle from her. He frowned when he realized it was still almost full.

"Don't worry, you're not about to take advantage of a drunken woman." Leah withdrew her feet from his lap and beckoned to him with a finger. "Come here, Sebastian Padilla. I've never had a millionaire make a pass at me before. It'd be rude to make me do all the chasing after this."

"Oh, you're quite right, we couldn't have that," he agreed, smiling at her coy smirk, and set the champagne bottle safely out of harm's way in the corner. He sat beside her, their shoulders touching lightly. "This what you had in mind?" he queried, looking down at her. "Or was it more like this?" One hand cupped her cheek, turning her face toward him before he leaned down and pressed his lips to hers.

*

Leah's eyes drifted shut as Sebastian's warm mouth moved slow and sure over hers. She parted her lips without conscious thought, felt his tongue stroke sensually into her mouth, and moaned deep in her throat.

"Fuck, Leah," Sebastian tore his mouth from hers and swore raggedly. "Fuck, hearing you make noises like that… all I can think about is what noises you'd make for me in bed."

She peered up at him through her lashes, lips parted and wet, breath coming quickly. "I bet I could get some pretty good noises out of you, too," some wicked imp made her say, and she put a hand on his thigh.

He did indeed make a very intriguing noise at that, a strangled sort of yelp, before hauling her suddenly up to sit facing him astride his lap, her slim-fitting skirt riding up almost to her hips. Strong hands landed on her ass, gripping the rounded flesh firmly as he yanked her hard against his body.

Leah's eyes just about rolled back in her head with pleasure. Sebastian made an impatient sound against her mouth before he yanked her skirt up the rest of the way, filling his hands with her ass, squeezing and kneading. He groaned as he explored, finding that she wore only a tiny thong - anything else would spoil the line of her dress, she'd told herself as she spent a fair chunk of her advance payment on some gorgeous new underwear. Money well spent, she concluded now, as Sebastian's fingers traced the lacy material in between her thighs.

What the hell am I doing? Leah wondered as Sebastian's mouth left hers and he ducked his head to kiss her neck, suckling the tender skin between his lips. The thought was fleeting, though, because it felt really good to be held against him like this, her breasts pressed against his chest, his strong hands kneading her ass, and a thick hardness poking at her through his pants, letting her know he was just as aroused by what they were doing as she was.

I'm having a damn good time, that's what, she thought and threw caution to the wind, putting one hand on the back of his neck, guiding his mouth closer to that sensitive spot just below her ear. The other arm she crooked up behind her and grasped the zipper on her dress.

The whirr of the zipper sliding down had Sebastian gasping, hips jolting against her even as he pulled back to look her in the eyes. "We doing this here?" he asked hoarsely.

"Good way to pass the time until we get rescued, huh?" Leah smirked at him. He chuckled before nodding, hands leaving her ass and gliding up her sides to grasp the short sleeves of her dress, pulling them down over her arms. Leaving his face almost pressed into her lush cleavage, spilling out over the lacy cups of her balconette bra.

"Oh my god, you have the most glorious tits," Sebastian groaned hoarsely before giving in and burying his face in them.

Leah chuckled softly and pulled her hands out of her sleeves, reaching up to grasp his head in both hands, holding him in there until he thought he might suffocate from sheer delight.

His six o'clock shadow had to be rasping against the delicate skin, but she seemed to be enjoying herself, letting out soft little gasps and whimpers as he mouthed at the upper slope of her bountiful breasts. It wasn't enough, though, he wanted more, so he moved his hand to the center of her back and unhooked the clip.

Leah's breasts spilled free as her bra loosened; impatiently she lifted her arms and dragged it off, flinging it aside carelessly. She hadn't even brought her arms back down before Sebastian latched onto one plump nipple, dragging it into his mouth and tonguing it impatiently, teasing it roughly up to a pouting, aching nub. Leah clung to his broad shoulders as he suckled, sensation zinging along her nerves, making her feel as though there was a direct line from her breast to her groin.

Sebastian switched his attention to her other breast, bringing his hand up to palm the one he'd just abandoned, catching her nipple between his finger and thumb and rolling it firmly, tugging until she moaned, testing just how much pressure she liked. Quite a lot, he quickly discovered, and used the edge of his teeth on her nipple to make her cry out, her fingers tightening in his thick hair. She wasn't trying to pull him off, though, and her hips grinding against his told him she was definitely enjoying what he was doing. He could feel heat and dampness through the layers of clothing between them; in fact, he suspected she might be leaving a wet spot on his trousers, not that he gave a damn about that. The mere thought of the slick juices he might find between her thighs had his cock hardening almost to the point of pain. He wanted to taste her. Right now.

"Stand up," he requested hoarsely, pulling back from her breast. "Stand up, I want to see you…"

Leah obeyed, scrambling to her feet on slightly shaky legs, putting her hands on the elevator's brass handrail to support herself. Sebastian reached up and eased her dress down over her hips; she brought her feet together briefly to kick out of it. Wearing only a lacy thong, she stood astride his body and smirked down at him. "Well?"

"You are absolutely magnificent," he told her with complete honesty, before he pushed himself up to his knees, wrapped his arms around her thighs, and pressed his face against her mound, mouthing over the damp lace.

"Oh my god." Leah had to tighten her grip on the handrail as Sebastian nuzzled the lacy scrap of her panties aside, tongue flicking out to taste her. She met her own eyes briefly in the mirrored wall, but it was too much; the woman looking back at her with kiss-swollen lips and a lustful expression on her face didn't look like her at all. She looked down instead, at Sebastian's dark head between her thighs, the open admiration in his eyes as he gazed up at her, his tongue parting delicate folds to find the hidden nub he sought.

Leah moaned long and loud as his hot tongue flicked over her clit. Sebastian smiled against her before setting up a rhythm of quick laps, tasting her musky juices as she shifted her legs further apart to grant him better access. One thumb held her panties out of the way while the fingers of the other hand snuck between her thighs to stroke a teasing circle around her entrance.

Her knees trembled, desperate whimpers spilling from her lips as he slowly pushed one finger deep inside her, right up to the last knuckle, before withdrawing completely and pressing back in again. The third time he pushed back in, there were two fingers.

It had been a long time since there had been anything other than her own fingers inside her, and Sebastian's felt oh so much better, thicker and longer, stronger than her own, able to achieve a far better angle than she could ever manage. He crooked them deftly in a beckoning gesture, drumming his fingertips on that sensitive spot deep inside her that was just too hard to reach on her own, and Leah's eyes rolled back in her head.

"Yes," she said gutturally, "don't stop…"

He didn't say a word, just kept working with his hot tongue and those long, talented fingers. She came in a sudden rush of sensation, her whole body quaking with the release, hands white-knuckled on the railing as she clung tightly to avoid just collapsing in a heap. She heard a wet sound and managed to force her eyes open enough to look down and see Sebastian licking at his fingers, making a pleased noise as he tasted her juices on them.

"Oh god, that's just too dirty," Leah panted. He grinned up at her and reached up to tug on her thighs, drawing her down towards him. She let her knees buckle and sagged rather ungracefully onto his lap, pressing her face against his neck. He was still almost fully dressed, she recognized vaguely, whereas she was down to nothing more than a thong he'd already proved might as well not be there for all the use it had been in covering her up.

Boneless with the pleasure still coursing through her body, Leah lay slumped against Sebastian for several minutes, her breathing and pulse gradually slowing to their normal pace. He seemed completely unbothered by having her lie on him, just nuzzling gentle kisses against her bare shoulder while one hand stroked slowly over her flank. He was still very much aroused, she could feel his erection pressing against her through his pants, but he seemed to be in no hurry about it. At last, she leaned back to look him in the eye.

"Want to do something about this?" Slipping her hand between them, she laid her hand over the swollen bar beneath his zipper.

"We could, but it might get messy. I don't have any condoms with me," Sebastian told her bluntly.

Leah snickered at that. "What, you? Really? Mr. I'm In Control Of Everything At All Times doesn't carry a condom in his wallet?"

"Certainly I do. Unfortunately, it's in my suite right along with my phone." He smiled up at her, unconcerned at her teasing. "Didn't figure I'd need it at a hotel where everything is on my tab anyway."

She smiled at that, nodding. "Well, it might just be your lucky day." Leaning sideways, she snagged the strap of the camera bag she'd been carrying around like an oversized purse. "Because I *am* prepared." From the side pocket where she kept spare memory cards, she produced a foil packet and held it up with a flourish.

"Alright, color me impressed," Sebastian's grin widened as he took the packet from her fingers. "You're sure you want to do this here?"

"Why not," Leah shrugged, glancing at the watch which was still on her wrist. "It's likely to be at least another hour before we get rescued. I can't think of any more fun ways to pass the time, can you?"

"Oh hell no."

She shifted off his legs to let him get up to undress, reaching for the bottle of champagne and taking a swig as she watched him unabashedly.

Sensing her appreciation, Sebastian didn't tear his clothes off as he would have preferred, but took his time, removing his cufflinks and stowing them in a pocket of his discarded jacket, slowly unbuttoning his shirt and spreading it open.

He knew how he looked, how women reacted to him, but it was rare that he felt a reciprocal attraction. Leah, with her curvaceous body and her fierce determination, made him react in a way he hadn't in longer than he cared to recall. Looking at her sprawled on the floor of the elevator, propped at her ease on one elbow drinking champagne from the bottle, he felt another moment's regret. He'd wanted his first time with her to be on silken sheets, not a hard floor; he wanted to take the time to explore her luscious body, her reactions to his lovemaking.

There was no reason he couldn't still have that, he thought, discarding the last of his clothes and standing before her naked and proud, watching her green eyes widen, pupils dilating with lust. No reason they couldn't go on up to his suite after the elevator was fixed and spend the rest of the night enjoying each other. And the following day for that matter, it was Sunday tomorrow and he'd booked in for Sunday night as well…

"Very nice," Leah's drawl interrupted his train of thought. "But do you know what to do with it?"

Sebastian had to laugh. She was so charmingly unaffected, not intimidated at all by his power and wealth. She hadn't backed down an inch when they were arguing over wedding arrangements and she clearly wasn't going to now either.

"Oh, I know what to do with it." He wrapped a hand around his cock and jacked it a few times, not that he needed it; he'd been hard as a rock ever since the elevator doors slid closed and shut them in together. Ripping the condom open, he rolled it on before going to his knees; he had to suppress a wince at the cold marble floor of the elevator, but Leah's ass was on it and she wasn't complaining, so he was damned if he'd show any discomfort. He allowed himself one more wistful thought of the luxurious, almost sinfully comfortable bed in his suite before moving between Leah's legs, pressing her thighs wide and gazing down at her as she lay back and relaxed, smiling up at him.

"Want some?" She offered the champagne bottle. He accepted it with a grin and took a gulp before leaning forward and tilting the bottle, pouring a little champagne between her breasts, leaning down to chase the droplets with his tongue.

Leah laughed and squirmed as the cool champagne dribbled over her skin, gasping as Sebastian's hot mouth followed, licking all around her breasts before his lips latched onto her nipple, suckling and tugging. Heat sparked through her again and she shuddered, arching up towards him.

"Sebastian," she gasped his name, reaching to touch his face, her hands landing on his shoulders. He was a work of art; she'd watched in sheer admiration as he disrobed, gazing at the solid muscles of his chest and shoulders, the flat planes of his belly. And his cock, that was certainly worth admiring too, thick and generous in length. "Please…" She wanted that cock inside her, filling her up.

"Yeah?" He hooked a hand under her knee, hitching it up, opening her wide to him. "You want it, Leah? Want a good fucking? How do you like it?" He was teasing the tip of his cock around her entrance now, wetting it with her juices, pressing in just a little way before pulling back again.

"Hard," she said breathlessly, trying to pull him closer, pull him into her. "Don't tease, Sebastian…"

"I got you," he promised, before his hips suddenly lunged forward and he drove deep inside her.

Leah's back bowed and she dug her fingernails into his shoulders, sobbing with pure pleasure as Sebastian's cock filled her tight channel.

He froze, lifting his head and cupping her cheek in his hand. "Leah, did I hurt you?"

"No!" She clawed at him, wrapping her legs around his lean hips, pressing her heels against his tightly muscled ass to urge him on. "More!"

He laughed roughly. "Oh, honey. I got more."

He did indeed, but the slippery marble floor meant he couldn't quite get the necessary leverage. Not until Leah flung her arms up over her head to brace herself against the wall, anyway, and then he hooked his elbows under her knees and lifted her ass into his lap.

"That's it," Sebastian grated out, hips pumping fast as he watched Leah's eyes flutter shut, her lips parted, soft little wails and moans spilling out of her. "That's it, honey. Come on. Let me feel you." He worked his arm further around her thigh, got his thumb over her clit, and started rubbing it in quick little circles. "I want to feel you come on me."

"You're not going to have to wait long if you keep doing that," Leah managed to gasp out. "Oh my god that's so good oh oh OOOHHHHHH!"

Sebastian was very glad she was so close to the edge; it meant he didn't have to try to cling to the fraying edges of his own sorely-tested control. As soon as he felt the rippling tug of Leah's internal muscles he sped up his pace, slamming into her roughly until he felt the familiar tingle at the base of his spine, the spreading heat of his climax as his seed jetted hotly from his cock into her welcoming heat.

"Christ." He stilled, leaning forward over Leah, breathing hard. "Oh, damn. Leah."

He felt her fingers against his face, stroking lightly over his cheek, her fingertips soft against the roughness of his sprouting stubble. Turning his head, he caught a finger with his lips, kissing it lightly before pulling slowly out of her.

*

"Ouch, fuck, my knees."

Leah had to giggle as Sebastian groaned painfully and collapsed to sit down. "Floor's pretty hard, huh?"

"Your ass alright?" He grinned at her as he removed the condom carefully and tied a knot to close it.

"Yeah." She felt kind of awkward lying there with her legs spread, so she sat up again and pressed her knees together primly, lifting them up to her chest as she leaned back against the wall. It was a defensive sort of posture, and Sebastian must have recognized that she felt a little vulnerable just at that moment, because he reached for his discarded jacket.

"Hey, want to put this around you?"

"Where did this sweet, considerate Sebastian come from?" she had to ask as she accepted the jacket and draped it around her shoulders. It smelled like him - expensive cologne, something woodsy and masculine. "I thought you were just the hard-nosed, ruthless businessman."

He looked at her thoughtfully as he pulled his boxers and pants back on, not bothering to zip the fly. "I guess it's the price of being in business. It's a cut-throat world out there - you show people that you've got a soft side and they'll stamp all over you. The people who matter to me know who I really am."

Leah wasn't entirely sure what to say to that, but she was saved from having to come up with a response by the speaker on the control panel suddenly crackling back into life.

"Hello, are you there?" the operator's voice said.

"Yes!" Instinctively, Leah clutched Sebastian's jacket closer around her, before realizing she was being ridiculous. The operator couldn't see her. *Or could she? Oh god, is there a camera in here?* She looked around frantically, peering up into the darkened corners of the roof, and saw a camera mounted there. There was no red light, but that might not mean anything. She caught Sebastian's eye and nodded toward the camera.

'Oh, shit,' he mouthed at her, looking startled.

"I've been able to locate a closer repair technician. He should be with you in about five minutes." The operator sounded bored to tears.

"Thank you," Sebastian said politely.

The speaker crackled and went silent again; Leah immediately burst out, "Oh my god, Sebastian, do you think that camera was recording?"

He shook his head at her. "I doubt it." Standing up, he peered up at the camera from as close as he could get to it. "Even if it was, there's hardly any light in here, and we were down on the floor. It's angled to pick stuff up at waist level or higher, I think. I'll get my people to look into it tomorrow and make sure that any footage there might be is destroyed, I promise."

She didn't feel reassured as she searched for her panties, finally finding them tossed behind her camera bag. Hastily scrambling back into them, she picked up her bra and put that back on too. Sebastian watched her as she shimmied back into her dress, crooking her hand up behind her to pull up the zipper. Sighing with audible regret, Sebastian zipped up his pants, picked up his shirt and shrugged back into it, fastening a few buttons.

"My zipper is stuck!" Leah shrieked, a note of panic in her voice.

"Okay, calm down," he said soothingly. "Let me have a look."

She turned her back to him, sweeping her hair over her shoulder to get it out of the way; it had tumbled free of the chignon during their lovemaking, falling almost halfway down her back in a thick mass of auburn waves Sebastian just wanted to bury his hands in. He reined the impulse, bending his head to peer at the zip of her dress in the dim light.

"I think a little bit of lace is caught in the teeth of the zipper." It was a tiny tag, too; he could barely get a hold on it between his large fingers. A couple of sharp yanks failed to get it loose.

"Try pulling it down instead of up," Leah suggested, trying to look back over her shoulder. Sebastian couldn't quite resist kissing her when she did that, and they lost another couple of minutes as she responded to him, her mouth opening eagerly under his.

The elevator lurching into motion startled them apart. Leah let out a panicked squeak; Sebastian jerked futilely at the zipper a couple more times before giving up.

"Put this on." He grabbed his jacket and threw it around her shoulders. Standing behind her as she hastily stuffed her arms through the sleeves, he wrapped his arm around her, holding the jacket closed to hide the fact that her dress was gaping away from her body in the front. Glancing around the elevator, he shrugged mentally over their discarded shoes - removing shoes was a reasonably natural thing to do in the circumstances - and froze in horror at the sight of the knotted condom still lying on the floor beside the empty foil packet. He'd just managed to dive on them, stuff the incriminating evidence into his pocket with a grimace of distaste, and put his arm back around Leah again, when the doors slid open.

"Evening, folks," the overall-clad repairman holding a large toolbox said with a friendly smile. "Apologies for the inconvenience. We'll have this old girl fixed in a jiffy and get you on your way to your rooms."

"I think we might just take one of the other elevators, actually," Leah said, and then realized she'd have to bend down to pick up her shoes and camera bag. She cast Sebastian a desperate look back over her shoulder.

"Good idea, darling." His free hand pushed at her elbow and she realized he was guiding her to fold her arms over her chest, to keep the jacket closed in front of her. "I'll get your things." He deftly scooped up the champagne bottle, her camera bag, and both pairs of their shoes before they left the elevator in all haste and turned to wait for another one.

Unfortunately, to complete Leah's humiliation, there were quite a few guests leaving the party now and heading upstairs.

"Are you wearing his jacket?" her friend Emma hissed, glancing incredulously from Leah to Sebastian and back again before grinning broadly. "You go, girl!" She delivered a sharp nudge to Leah's ribs.

There wasn't a lot Leah could say. She certainly couldn't get out when Emma and her husband did on the sixth floor, because she would have had to hand Sebastian's jacket back and that was completely out of the question. She just smiled tightly, let Sebastian put his arm around her again, and bore the surreptitious looks and whispers until at last the elevator reached the top floor.

"Good night," Sebastian said to one of the senior executives from his firm, and got a knowing wink before the man took himself off. "This way." He guided Leah toward his suite, letting them in and closing the door firmly behind them.

"Okay, that may have been the most embarrassing thing that's *ever* happened to me," Leah groaned as the door clicked shut. "The way everyone was looking at us! Like they knew exactly what we'd been up to!"

"I'm pretty sure they didn't think we'd been banging in the elevator," Sebastian said. Tactfully he didn't mention Leah's messed-up hair and kiss-swollen lips. It was pretty obvious that they'd been up to *something*.

"No, they just think we're going to bang now!"

"Aren't we?"

The quiet question cut through her panic, froze the words on her lips. Staring at him, Leah licked her lips uncertainly.

"I mean, we don't have to. You can leave any time you like. But I was hoping I'd be able to take my time with you the second time around. And not kill my knees on a hard marble floor while I'm doing so." Sebastian shrugged, trying to look casual and suspecting he was failing badly. The truth was that the hasty coupling in the elevator had only whetted his appetite.

*

Leah turned away from the intense gaze Sebastian was leveling at her and looked around, trying to buy some time to think. The suite was just as glamorous as she'd expected, all ornate antique furniture which actually looked as though it might be comfortable to use. The bed was an actual four-poster, made up with white sheets she was pretty sure weren't the same grade as the ones in her standard-issue room.

"Nice place," she said, trying to keep her tone light.

"Leah." His voice was soft, but she could tell from the tone that he wasn't going to let her deflect. "Do you want to go? It's okay if you do." His hand touched her elbow lightly, and she could swear she felt the heat of it even through his jacket, which she was still wearing. "This is… the elevator… I feel like I rushed things."

She grinned, seeing the funny side. "It was certainly what you'd call a quickie, huh?" Turning to look up at him, she saw desire that matched her own in his eyes, and she threw caution to the wind. "No, Sebastian. I don't want to go." Deliberately, she shrugged her shoulders, letting his jacket slide down until it slipped off her arms, and then tossed it negligently at a nearby chair. "But you're going to have to have another go at this zipper, or I'm gonna be stuck in this dress."

Sebastian let out a gasp of relief. "Sure! Yes, of course." He grasped the zipper tag in his fingers and gave it a determined yank. The tiny piece of metal popped right off.

"Oh, shit." Giving up, he just grasped the dress and wrenched. The recalcitrant zipper tore right open.

"My dress!" Leah squawked with horror at the sound of ripping fabric.

"I'll buy you a new one." He was already easing it down over her hips, catching her panties to pull them down too.

She shook her head with a grin, looking back over her shoulder at him. "It was a designer knockoff anyway, Sebastian. I just hoped to get more than one use out of it."

He unhooked her bra as she stepped out of the dress, placing slow sensual kisses on her shoulders as he drew the straps down her arms. "Then I'll buy you the real deal. You deserve designer."

Leah laughed. "Oh, Sebastian. I doubt that designer even makes dresses in my size. I'm pretty sure they top out at size six."

His brow furrowed, and she shook her head, realizing he genuinely had no idea what she was talking about. "Never mind." She really didn't give a damn about the dress, not when Sebastian was looking at her like that and there was a bed only a few steps away. Catching his hand in hers, she pulled, leading him towards that decadent-looking bed. "I've never had sex on a four-poster bed before."

"No?" Sebastian allowed her to change the subject, though he mentally filed it for later. "The posts can be very useful."

She looked up at him with a bemused expression. "Useful for what?"

"Oh, I can think of lots of things." His grin was wicked. "Tying you up while I spank that beautiful bottom, for example?" His pat on her ass wasn't firm enough to be called a smack, but Leah still squeaked, her cheeks blushing scarlet. "Or keeping you restrained while I make you come over and over again with my tongue until you're screaming for mercy?"

"You are *outrageous*." Leah was sure she was fire red all over.

Sebastian chuckled, his gaze never leaving hers as he stripped his shirt off and shucked his pants and boxers. He was erect again, cock standing out proudly toward her as he stalked forward. "I think you like outrageous," he taunted lightly, stopping just before their bodies met. She swayed towards him unconsciously, breasts almost brushing his chest, his cock nudging against the softness of her belly. "I just asked you up here for a drink. You're the one who jumped me in the elevator."

"You!" Leah's mouth opened wide with shock, until she saw the teasing glint in his eye. Laughing, she let herself topple backward onto the bed, pulling Sebastian with her. He came more than willingly, catching himself from landing heavily on her with his arms braced on either side of her body. He still landed on her, though, his muscled chest against her plump breasts, and suddenly their mouths were crashing together again, Leah's arms winding around Sebastian's neck, her fingers sinking into his thick hair, nails scratching at his scalp.

In the back of her mind, Leah had wondered if the intense chemistry she'd felt in the elevator with Sebastian had been real, or if it had just been some sort of fluke, a reaction caused by the circumstances of being trapped together.

Now, she knew it was something more. Heat raced through her body again as Sebastian's hand came up to cup her breast, thumb flicking over her nipple, his tongue playing a teasing game with hers. Deliberately, she bent her knees and rocked her hips against him, making a hungry sound in her throat as his hard cock slid along the slick channel between her thighs.

"Jesus, woman, are you trying to kill me?" Sebastian threw his head back and groaned, the cords standing out in his neck as he fought for control. He wanted nothing more at that moment than to plunge deep inside Leah's warm, willing body and just take his pleasure. "I promised myself I was gonna take my time with you this time around…"

"Shut up and fuck me," she demanded, delirious with lust.

He almost did, until he caught himself and remembered. "Condom." He pulled back, away from her grasping hands, and dove for the bathroom and his shaving kit. He fumbled it open, grabbing for the strip of foil packets he knew he'd put in there.

Hurrying back to the bedroom, he stopped short at the end of the bed, taking in the spectacular sight of Leah taking matters into her own hands, quite literally. One hand was cupped over her breast, plucking at a swollen nipple, the other between her parted thighs, forefinger tracing a lazy circle around her glistening clit.

"You really are trying to kill me," Sebastian said, his mouth dry, his fingers shaking as he ripped open a packet and rolled the latex sheath onto his straining erection. "But damn, I'll die a happy man."

Leah laughed, soft and husky, watching him from under lowered eyelids. "You gonna just stand there or are you gonna come and help me out?"

"Oh, I can help you out all right." The bed dipped as he climbed on, but instead of kneeling between her thighs as she'd hoped, he moved to one side, patting her hip lightly. "Turn over."

She licked her lips at the thought of him taking her from behind, rolled eagerly to her stomach, and pushed herself up on hands and knees, presenting her ass in the air.

"Oh, angel," Sebastian's already deep voice lowered further as he smoothed his hands reverently over her rounded bottom. "Oh, that is absolutely magnificent. *You're* magnificent."

Leah smiled into the pillow and deliberately wiggled her ass. "Can you handle this booty?"

"I know exactly what to do with all this spectacular booty." His hands settled on her hips, grasping firmly as he moved closer. His cock pushed up against her ass for a moment, making her suck in a shocked breath, before he leaned forward and it slid down between her thighs, rubbing along her crotch. Instinctively she rocked her hips, rubbing against him, enjoying the slide and rub over her already-slick folds.

Sebastian's hands tightened on her hips in a silent instruction to be still. She had to clench her fists in the sheets and focus in order to obey, but was quickly rewarded as she felt the thick head of his cock nudging into her soaked passage.

"Yes," she said throatily into the pillow as he pressed in a little deeper, strong hands pulling her back into the thrust. "Oh my god, yes!"

"I didn't even ask you yet," he said, amused, leaning down to press a kiss against her spine. "Is this okay?"

"It's a lot better than okay." He was pressing deeper still, stretching delicate tissues. He must be all the way inside her now. Surely. Leah yelped in protest as he pulled back a little.

"Easy." His voice sounded strained, his breath warm against her back. "Damn, Leah, you're so tight…"

She didn't want to admit that it had been a while. The way he felt inside her was so good, anyway, she just pressed her forehead against the pillow and pushed back against him in a silent demand that he continue. That he give her more, give her all he had, fill her up completely.

Sebastian obeyed Leah's silent plea. He took it slow, not wanting to hurt her; she really was tight and at this angle his penetration was even more intimate than the first time, pressing on some very sensitive spots deep inside her. Finally he was fully seated, right to the hilt, the very end of his cock just brushing her cervix.

Leah was moaning continuously, her hips rotating in tight little circles, fingers grasping at the sheets. Sebastian felt a bit like clawing at the bed himself and had to make himself relax his tight grip on her hips before he left bruises.

She made protesting noises, trying to shove back against him, wanting, needing him to be rougher with her.

"Please!" burst from her, a frantic cry.

"I got you, I got you," Sebastian promised. One hand settled on her shoulder, bracing her. His other hand curved around in front of her, fingers seeking and finding her clit. "I got you, angel. You gonna let me feel you come again?" His fingertips began to scissor rapidly as he set up a steady, driving rhythm with his hips. "This what you need?"

It was exactly what she needed; it was perfect. Leah sobbed with ecstasy, bracing herself against Sebastian's pounding thrusts. He was slamming into her with all his strength even as his fingers worked over her clit, and it was absolutely the best thing that had ever happened to her in her whole entire life. He was grunting and gasping, pounding hard against her, and it was so sexy and dirty and wonderful that she just let herself go, screaming at the top of her lungs as the most intense climax she'd ever experienced crashed through her.

Sebastian didn't let up. He fucked her right through it and kept on going, letting go of her clit when she shoved at his hand because she was getting too sensitive… only to grab onto her breast, tugging and squeezing almost cruelly at her nipple. Both nipples, when he let go of her shoulder and dropped that hand around in front of her too.

To Leah, it seemed to go on for a blissful eternity, her pleasure cresting in waves and crashing through her. She was barely aware of Sebastian finally stiffening behind her with a low, harsh groan, his eyes closing as he surged inside her for one final time.

Leah collapsed to the mattress in a boneless heap when Sebastian finally pulled out of her. He winced and dropped to lie beside her, reaching out to drape his arm over her.

"You okay?" he checked, kissing her shoulder gently.

"Unf." She opened one green eye and peered at him. "No. I'm dead. You have killed me with sex."

Smiling with relief that she was still teasing him, he mustered the energy to get off the bed to go and clean up in the bathroom. Leah had rearranged her limbs into a slightly more comfortable-looking position when he returned, though she was still lying on her front; he gazed admiringly at the round fullness of her ass for a few moments before reaching for the folded coverlet at the foot of the bed and pulling it up over her.

"You okay with me staying?" Leah roused enough to ask.

Sebastian gave her a puzzled stare. "Why wouldn't I be?"

She opened her mouth to say she thought he was the type of man who wouldn't want to risk his women getting too close, wouldn't want them staying the night in his bed. But then, she'd already misjudged him quite a few times, and he might get offended.

"No reason," she said. Her eyelids were drifting, heavy with sleep; she felt him kiss her cheek softly and smiled.

"Sleep, Leah. I'll see you in the morning."

*

Leah woke in the early light of morning desperate to pee. Disorientated for a moment, not knowing where the hell she was as she opened her eyes to an unfamiliar room, the heavy weight on her stomach made her glance to her left.

Sebastian lay there, fast asleep, firm lips slightly parted, stubble blackening his hard jaw, his arm slung comfortably, possessively, over her.

Memories of the previous night came crashing back and Leah froze, wild-eyed for a little while, wondering if he would wake up if she moved. At last the urgent demand of her bladder got to her and she very, very carefully wiggled out from under his heavy arm. The only thing she could cover herself with was the coverlet lying over him as well and picking that up would almost certainly wake him up, so she made a hasty nude dash to the bathroom.

Washing her hands, she winced at her reflection in the mirror. Her hair was all over the place, her eye makeup had turned into a panda mask, her lips looked swollen and red, and she had pink patches on her chin from stubble rash.

In short, she looked a fright, and there wasn't a lot she could do about it. She dampened a washcloth and tried to clean her face off as best she could, finger-combed her hair, and finally gained the courage to go back into the bedroom, this time wrapped in a large bath sheet from the heated towel rail.

Sebastian was still soundly asleep.

Irresolute, Leah stood watching him, the old familiar doubts and uncertainties creeping in. He couldn't really be interested in her. He was rich, handsome, charming; he could have anyone he wanted. She'd been a challenge, that was all, because she didn't immediately fall at his feet. Now that he'd had what he wanted he'd lose interest. Better to slip quietly away now rather than face the humiliation of being asked to leave, of seeing the disgust in his eyes when he looked at her in the cold light of day.

Looking around, her gaze fell on the ruined dress on the floor and her lips twisted wryly. Well, she certainly couldn't wear that on her walk of shame back to her room. Which was best done as quickly as possible, hopefully before any of the other guests saw her. Her eyes fell on Sebastian's discarded dress shirt and she snatched it up quickly. He was nearly a foot taller than she was and broad through the chest; she shouldn't burst out of it and it would at least cover her butt and the tops of her thighs. Tiptoeing around the room to collect her underwear, shoes, and camera bag, she cast one last regretful look at the sleeping man in the bed before creeping out and closing the door behind her as quietly as she could manage.

*

Sebastian woke cold and alone, the soft scent of Leah teasing in his nostrils… but the woman herself was gone, leaving only a torn dress behind. He clenched his fists and swore under his breath. Had he said something, done something to put her off, make her think she had to leave without a word, without even a god damned note? He'd been looking forward to waking up beside her, loving her again, maybe taking a shower and ordering a room service breakfast to eat in bed together.

Obviously she hadn't felt the same way. She thought he was just a playboy, she'd made that pretty clear, but he wasn't playing around. Leah was the most beautiful, fascinating, challenging woman he'd ever met, and he wanted a lot more from her than just a single night.

Getting out of the mussed bed, he headed for the shower, his stride purposeful. He'd convince Leah he was worth taking a chance on.

He had to.

*

Leah opened the fridge and surveyed its contents despondently. Half a carton of Chinese takeout of indeterminate age, a bottle of sriracha, an essentially empty jar of mayo, and some wilted lettuce in a plastic bag didn't look like a particularly appetizing dinner. Blowing out her cheeks, she closed the door and considered going out to get something. Or maybe just choosing from her extensive selection of takeout menus and ordering in.

She was debating between pizza and Thai when there was a loud knock at the door. Looking up in surprise, she headed over to peer through the peephole and almost died on the spot when she saw Sebastian's handsome face. Leaning against the door, she pressed a hand to her chest, where her heart was doing a great impression of a galloping horse, and tried to calm herself down.

"Leah?" His deep voice on the other side of the door set her heart racing again. "Are you there?"

Slowly, her fingers shaking, she reached up to slide off the chain and open the deadbolt. Pulling the door open a few inches, she looked at him in uncertain silence. He was dressed casually, in jeans and a black button-down shirt that made him look darkly handsome and damn near edible.

"Hey." Sebastian shuffled his feet awkwardly before pulling a hand from behind his back and almost thrusting a bunch of bright yellow daffodils into her chest.

Even more startled, Leah took the flowers instinctively. "What… what are you doing here? How did you know where I live?"

"That was a bit of a pain to track down, actually," Sebastian admitted, shoving his hands in his pockets and rocking back on his heels. "I had to wait until Sal and Heather got to the hotel in Hawaii and then talk Heather into giving me your address."

Her jaw dropped. "You *what?* You interrupted them on their *honeymoon?*"

"I couldn't figure out another way to get in touch with you quickly!" he defended himself. "Since you apparently don't read your email… I got your email address off your website."

"It's Sunday, I was taking a day off. What was so urgent, anyway?"

"The best night of my life, and the desperate need to ask you for a repeat?" Sebastian chewed on the corner of his lip, eying Leah uncertainly. "Why did you run out on me this morning?" It came out more plaintive than he would have liked, but the hell with it. She had him wrapped around her little finger already; he was pretty sure she'd figure that out soon enough.

The small smile dawning on Leah's lips, the light brightening in her eyes, gave him hope. He took a step forward, hooked his arm around her waist, and pulled her closer, heedless of the flowers being crushed between them.

"I was really disappointed," he told her, a scant inch separating their lips. Hers parted slightly, her eyelids lowering.

"Were you?" Her voice was definitely a little breathless.

"Mm-hm. I'd been having wonderful dreams about ways we might make use of those other two condoms I found."

"Like… a water balloon fight?" A smirk grew on her lips as she made the suggestion.

Sebastian couldn't help it. He threw his head back and roared with laughter. Leah was giggling against his chest by the time he managed to stop, the flowers now a hopelessly crushed mess between them.

"I am crazy about you," he told her sincerely, framing her face in both his hands before kissing her slowly and tenderly, leaving her in no doubt at all that one night was never, ever going to be enough.

She smiled up at him when he let her go. "Do you think your enthusiasm for my company might extend to taking me out to dinner? The contents of my fridge are probably overdue for a decent burial, to be honest."

Ignoring the yellow pollen now dusting the front of his clean shirt, Sebastian took her hand in his, lifted it to his lips to kiss. "Of course, angel. Whatever you want."

~   **The End**   ~

ABOUT THE AUTHOR

Caitlyn Lynch is an Australian author who loves writing about sexy people finding their happily ever after together!

You can connect with her on her website

www.caitlynlynch.com

www.ingramcontent.com/pod-product-compliance
Lightning Source LLC
Chambersburg PA
CBHW071003120726
47910CB00004B/1356